PENGUIN CLASSICS
Maigret and the Tall Woman

'I love reading Simenon. He makes me think of Chekhov'
– William Faulkner

'A truly wonderful writer . . . marvellously readable – lucid, simple, absolutely in tune with the world he creates'
– Muriel Spark

'Few writers have ever conveyed with such a sure touch, the bleakness of human life'   – A. N. Wilson

'One of the greatest writers of the twentieth century . . . Simenon was unequalled at making us look inside, though the ability was masked by his brilliance at absorbing us obsessively in his stories'   – *Guardian*

'A novelist who entered his fictional world as if he were part of it'   – Peter Ackroyd

'The greatest of all, the most genuine novelist we have had in literature'   – André Gide

'Superb . . . The most addictive of writers . . . A unique teller of tales'   – *Observer*

'The mysteries of the human personality are revealed in all their disconcerting complexity'   – Anita Brookner

'A writer who, more than any other crime novelist, combined a high literary reputation with popular appeal'
– P. D. James

'A supreme writer . . . Unforgettable vividness'– *Independent*

'Compelling, remorseless, brilliant'   – John Gray

'Extraordinary masterpieces of the twentieth century'
– John Banville

ABOUT THE AUTHOR

Georges Simenon was born on 12 February 1903 in Liège, Belgium, and died in 1989 in Lausanne, Switzerland, where he had lived for the latter part of his life. Between 1931 and 1972 he published seventy-five novels and twenty-eight short stories featuring Inspector Maigret.

Simenon always resisted identifying himself with his famous literary character, but acknowledged that they shared an important characteristic:

> My motto, to the extent that I have one, has been noted often enough, and I've always conformed to it. It's the one I've given to old Maigret, who resembles me in certain points . . . 'understand and judge not'.

Penguin is publishing the entire series of Maigret novels.

GEORGES SIMENON

Maigret and the Tall Woman

Translated by DAVID WATSON

PENGUIN BOOKS

PENGUIN CLASSICS

UK | USA | Canada | Ireland | Australia
India | New Zealand | South Africa

Penguin Books is part of the Penguin Random House group of companies
whose addresses can be found at global.penguinrandomhouse.com

Penguin
Random House
UK

First published in French as *Maigret et la Grande Perche* by Presses de la Cité 1951
This translation first published 2016
012

Copyright © Georges Simenon Limited, 1951
Translation copyright © David Watson, 2016
GEORGES SIMENON ® Simenon.tm
MAIGRET ® Georges Simenon Limited

Set in Dante MT Std 12.5/15pt
Typeset in India by Thomson Digital Pvt Ltd, Noida, Delhi

Printed and bound in Great Britain by Clays Ltd, Elcograf S.p.A.

ISBN: 978-0-241-27738-6

www.greenpenguin.co.uk

MIX
Paper from
responsible sources
FSC® C018179

Penguin Random House is committed to a
sustainable future for our business, our readers
and our planet. This book is made from Forest
Stewardship Council® certified paper.

Maigret and the Tall Woman

1.

Where Maigret meets an old acquaintance who has settled down in her own way, and the story of Sad Freddie and a possible corpse

Maigret read the docket that the office clerk had had the visitor fill out and handed to him:

> Ernestine, aka 'La Grande Perche' (née Micou, now Jussiaume), the tall woman you arrested seventeen years ago in Rue de la Lune, and who stripped b— naked just to taunt you, requests the honour of speaking to you urgently about a matter of the utmost importance.

Maigret cast a sidelong glance at old Joseph to check whether he had read the note, but the white-haired clerk was giving nothing away. He was probably the only person in the offices of the Police Judiciaire that morning who was not in shirt-sleeves, and for the first time in all these years the inspector asked himself what bizarre regulation compelled this venerable old man to wear a heavy chain with an enormous medallion around his neck.

There are days like that, when you ask yourself silly questions. Maybe it was the late-summer heat; maybe it was the holiday atmosphere, which stopped you taking anything seriously. The windows were wide open, and the rumble of Paris vibrated in the office, where, before Joseph had turned up, Maigret had been busy following a wasp with his eyes as it flew round and round and crashed into the ceiling at exactly the same spot each time. A good half of the Police Judiciaire was at the seaside or in the country. Lucas was sporting a panama hat which, on him, looked like a native's hut or a lampshade. The commissioner had headed off the day before to the Pyrenees, as he did every year.

'Is she drunk?' Maigret asked the clerk.

'I don't think so, sir.'

Because there are women who, after a few too many drinks, like to go and make disclosures to the police.

'Nervous?'

'She asked if it would take long, and I replied that I wasn't even sure if you would see her. She sat down in a corner of the waiting room and started reading the newspaper.'

Maigret couldn't remember the name Micou, or Jussiaume, or the 'Grande Perche' nickname, but he had a clear recollection of Rue de la Lune on a hot day like today, when the bitumen feels soft under the soles of your shoes and Paris is impregnated with the stink of tar.

A little street down by Porte Saint-Denis, full of shady hotels and shops selling pastries and waffles. He wasn't a detective chief inspector at the time. The women wore flapper dresses and had their hair shaved at the neck. Looking for information on the girl, he had gone into two or three of the local bars and might have drunk the odd Pernod or two. He could almost smell them again, along

4

with the whiff of armpits and feet that pervaded the tiny hotel. The room was on the third or fourth floor. He had gone to the wrong door at first and had come face to face with a black man, sitting on his bed playing the accordion, probably a musician in a dance hall. Unperturbed, the man had indicated the room next door with a jerk of his chin.

'Come in!'

A husky voice. The voice of someone who had drunk and smoked too much. Then, by the window looking out on the courtyard well, a tall young woman in a blue dressing gown frying a chop on a spirit stove.

She was as tall as Maigret, perhaps taller. She scrutinized him from head to toe with no flicker of emotion, then said straight away:

'You a cop?'

He found the wallet and the banknotes on top of the mirror-fronted wardrobe, and she didn't flinch.

'My girlfriend did it.'

'Which girlfriend?'

'I don't know her name. We call her Lulu.'

'Where is she?'

'Find her. That's your job.'

'Get dressed and come with me.'

It was a petty case of a whore stealing from a client, but at Quai des Orfèvres it was a matter of some importance, not so much because of the money involved, though it was a tidy sum, but because the victim was a major cattle dealer from Charente who had already got his parliamentary deputy involved.

'Are you going to let me eat my chop first?'

The tiny room had only one chair in it. He remained standing while the girl ate, taking her time, paying no attention to him, as if he simply didn't exist.

She must have been about twenty at the time. She was pale, with colourless eyes and a long, bony face. He could see her now, picking her teeth with a matchstick and pouring boiling water into her coffee-pot.

'I asked you to get dressed.'

It was hot, and the smell of the hotel was bothering him. Had she sensed his unease?

Calmly, she took off her dressing gown, her slip and her underwear and, naked as the day she was born, stretched out on the bed and lit a cigarette.

'I'm waiting!' he said impatiently, forcing himself to look the other way.

'Me too.'

'I have an arrest warrant.'

'So arrest me, then.'

'Get dressed and come with me.'

'I'm fine as I am.'

It was a ridiculous situation. She was calm, passive, with just a glint of irony in those colourless eyes.

'You said you were arresting me. That's fine by me. But don't ask me to give you a hand. This is my place. I'm hot and I'm allowed to be naked if I want. So if you insist that I come with you just as I am, I have no problem with that.'

He repeated himself at least ten times:

'Get dressed.'

And perhaps because of the paleness of her skin, perhaps because of the squalid décor, he thought that he had never seen a woman quite as naked as she was. He tried throwing her clothes on the bed, threatening her, then persuading her, all to no avail.

In the end he went downstairs to summon a couple of police officers, and the scene descended into farce. They had to forcibly wrap the girl up in a blanket and carry her, like a parcel, down the narrow stairs, while all the doors opened as they went past.

He had never seen her again after that. He had never even heard her mentioned.

'Send her in,' he sighed.

He recognized her straight away. She didn't seem to have changed at all. The same long, pale face, the washed-out eyes, the wide, heavily lipsticked mouth that looked like an open wound. And in her expression he could see the cool irony of those who have seen so much that nothing seems terribly important to them any more. She was wearing a respectable dress, a light-green straw hat and a pair of gloves.

'Are you still annoyed with me?'

He sucked on his pipe and didn't reply.

'Can I sit down? I knew that you'd been promoted, which is why our paths never crossed again. Am I allowed to smoke?'

She took a cigarette from her bag and lit it.

'No hard feelings, but let me tell you straight away that back then I was in the right. I got sent down for a year, which I didn't deserve. There really was a Lulu, who you didn't bother to look for. We were together when we met that fat moneybags. He chose the both of us, but once he'd had a good look at me he told me to clear off because he didn't like skinny girls. I waited in the corridor, and then, an hour later, Lulu slipped me his wallet to stash away.'

'What happened to her?'

'She opened a small restaurant in the Midi about five years ago. I just wanted to show you that everyone makes mistakes now and then.'

'Is that why you came?'

'No. I came to tell you about Alfred. If he knew I was here he'd think I'm crazy. I could have gone to see Inspector Boissier, who knows him well.'

'Who is Alfred?'

'My husband. He really is my husband – we got married at the registry office and in church too, because he's still religious. Inspector Boissier arrested him a couple of times. One time, he got five years in Fresnes.'

Her voice sounded almost rasping.

'The name Jussiaume maybe won't mean anything to you, but his nickname will ring a bell. It's often been mentioned in the papers. He's Sad Freddie.'

'The safe-cracker?'

'Yes.'

'Have you had a fight?'

'No. I'm not here for the reason you think. It's not my style. So, you know who Alfred is now?'

Maigret had never seen him; more precisely, had only ever caught sight of him in the corridor when the burglar was waiting to be questioned by Boissier. He vaguely recalled a puny little man with darting eyes, wearing clothes that seemed two sizes too big for his scrawny body.

'Of course, we don't have the same opinion of him,' she said. 'He's not got a lot going for him, but he's more interesting than you imagine. I've been living with him for twelve years now and I'm starting to get to know him better.'

'Where is he?'

'I'm getting there, don't worry. I don't know where he is, but he's managed to get himself into a right old mess, and that's why I'm here. I need you to trust me, and I realize that's asking a lot.'

He looked at her curiously; her plain speaking was somehow appealing. She wasn't putting it on, wasn't trying to impress him. She might have been struggling to get to the point, but that was because what she had to say was genuinely complicated.

Nevertheless, there was a major barrier between them, and it was this barrier she was trying to break down, so that he didn't get the wrong idea.

Maigret had had very little to do with Sad Freddie personally and so knew no more about him than what he had heard around the office. He was something of a celebrity and had been rather romanticized by the newspapers because of his colourful exploits.

He had worked for the safe-makers Planchart for many years and was one of their top experts. Even then he was a sad, dour character; his health was poor and he suffered periodic fits of epilepsy.

Boissier would probably be able to fill Maigret in on the circumstances of his leaving Planchart.

Whatever had happened, instead of installing safes, he had turned to breaking into them.

'Was he still in full-time employment when you met him?'

'Certainly not. It wasn't me that led him astray, if that's what you're thinking. He did odd jobs, sometimes a bit of work for a locksmith, but I quickly cottoned on to what he was really up to.'

'Are you sure you wouldn't rather talk to Boissier?'

'He takes care of burglaries, doesn't he? You're the one in charge of murders.'

'Has Alfred killed someone?'

'Listen, inspector, I think we'll get there quicker if you just let me talk. Call Alfred what you like, but he wouldn't kill anyone for all the gold in the world. It may seem stupid to say this about a man like him, but he is a sensitive type who can cry at the drop of a hat. I should know. Some would say that he is soft. Maybe that's the reason why I fell in love with him.'

She looked at him calmly. She had said these last words without emphasis, but with a certain pride in her voice.

'If you knew everything that went on in his head you'd be amazed. But no matter. As far as you're concerned he's just a thief. He's been caught before and spent five years inside. I didn't miss a single visiting day and the whole time he was locked up I had to take up my old profession, at the risk of getting into trouble, because I wasn't registered, and you still needed to be on the books to work on the street in those days.

'He keeps hoping he'll pull off one big job, then we can go and live in the country. It's been his dream since he was little.'

'Where do you live?'

'Quai de Jemmapes, just opposite the Saint-Martin Lock. We have two rooms above a bar painted green. It's quite handy because of the telephone.'

'Is Alfred there right now?'

'No. I've already told you I don't know where he is. You just have to believe me. He pulled a job, not last night but the night before.'

'And he's run away?'

'Bear with me, inspector. You'll understand soon enough why what I have to tell you is important. You know those people who buy a lottery ticket for every draw, don't you? Some of them go without food in order to buy the ticket, in the belief that in a few days' time they'll be rich. Well, Alfred is like that. There are dozens of safes in Paris that he installed and knows like the back of his hand. Usually people buy safes to lock away money and jewellery.'

'He hopes he will hit the jackpot?'

'Exactly.'

She shrugged her shoulders, as if she were talking about some innocent childhood enthusiasm. Then she added:

'He's had no luck. Mostly he's found title deeds that are impossible to sell or business documents. One time he did find a large sum of money, large enough to allow him to live in peace for the rest of his days, but that time Boissier arrested him.'

'Were you with him? Do you act as his lookout?'

'No. He didn't want that. In the beginning he'd tell me where he was doing the job, and I'd arrange it so that I was in the vicinity. When he realized, he didn't confide in me any more.'

'He's worried you might be caught?'

'Maybe. But probably for superstitious reasons as well. You see, even though we live together, he's essentially a lone wolf; he can go two days without saying a single word. When I see him go out in the evening with his bicycle, I know what he's up to.'

That was a detail that had stuck in Maigret's mind. Some newspapers had dubbed Alfred Jussiaume the 'burglar with the bike'.

'He has this idea that a man riding a bicycle at night will be inconspicuous, especially if he has a toolbox over his shoulder. People will think that he's on his way to work. You see that I'm talking to you as a friend here.'

Maigret again wondered what she had come to his office for. When she took out another cigarette, he offered her a light.

'Today's Thursday. The night of Tuesday to Wednesday, Alfred went out on a job.'

'Did he tell you what he was doing?'

'He's been going out at the same time for a few nights. That's usually a give-away. Before breaking into a house or an office, he sometimes spends a week watching the premises to get to know the habits of the people there.'

'And to make sure no one will be around?'

'No. That doesn't bother him. I think he even prefers to work when someone is about rather than when the place is empty. He can move around without making a sound. Loads of times he's slipped into bed next to me at night and I hadn't even noticed he'd come home.'

'Do you know where he was working the night before last?'

'I just know that it was somewhere in Neuilly. And I only discovered that by accident. The day before, when he got home, he told me that the police had asked to see his papers; they must have thought he was up to no good, because they stopped him at the Bois de Boulogne, near the spot where women go to pick up trade.

'"Where was that?" I asked him.

'"Behind the Botanical Garden. I was on my way back from Neuilly."

'So the night before last, when he went off with his tools, I realized that he was off on a job.'

'Had he been drinking?'

'He doesn't drink or smoke. I wouldn't allow it. He lives in fear of having a fit and he is always deeply ashamed when it happens to him in the middle of the street, with lots of people gathering round and feeling sorry for him. Before he left he told me:

'"I think this one will be our ticket to the country."'

Maigret had started taking notes, and surrounding them with doodles.

'What time did he leave Quai de Jemmapes?'

'Around eleven in the evening, like on the previous days.'

'So he must have got to Neuilly at about midnight.'

'Probably. He never cycles very fast. On the other hand, there's not much traffic at that time of night.'

'When did you see him again?'

'I didn't.'

'And did you think something must have happened to him?'

'He telephoned me.'

'When?'

'At five in the morning. I wasn't asleep. I was worried. He always has this fear of having a fit in the street, but I always think it could happen while he is on a job, do you understand? I heard the telephone ring in the bar downstairs. Our room is directly above it. The bar owners didn't get up, so I guessed it was for me and went down. I could tell from his voice that there had been a hitch. He was whispering:

'"Is that you?"

'"Yes."

'"Are you alone?"

'"Yes. Where are you?"

'"Next to Gare du Nord, in a little café.

'"Listen, Tine" – he always calls me Tine – "I have to make myself scarce for a while."

'"Were you spotted?"

'"That's not it. I don't know. A guy saw me, but I don't think he was from the police."

'"Do you have the money?"

'"No, it happened before I finished."

'"What happened?"

'"I was working on the lock when my torch lit up a face in a corner of the room. I thought someone had come in without a sound and was looking at me. But then I noticed that the eyes were dead."'

She observed Maigret.

'I'm sure he wasn't lying. If he had killed someone, he would have told me. I'm not spinning you a line. I could tell he was close to fainting at the other end of the phone. He is so afraid of death . . .'

'Who was it?'

'I don't know. He didn't give any detail. He seemed in a hurry to hang up. He was afraid of being overheard. He told me he was going to catch a train a quarter of an hour later . . .'

'For Belgium?'

'Probably, as he was next to Gare du Nord. I checked a timetable. There is a train at five forty-five.'

'And you don't know which café he was ringing from?'

'I wandered round the area yesterday, asking questions, but drew a blank. They must have thought I was a jealous wife, because no one wanted to tell me anything.'

'So basically all he told you was that there was a dead body in the room where he was working?'

'I got a bit more out of him. He said it was a woman, and that her chest was covered with blood, and that she was holding a telephone receiver in her hand.'

'Is that all?'

'No. Just as he was about to get away – and I can just imagine the state he was in! – a car pulled up outside the gate—'

'He actually said "gate"?'

'Yes, I distinctly remember him using the word. It struck me. Someone got out and headed for the door. While the man came into the hallway, Alfred slipped out of the house through the window.'

'And his tools?'

'He left them behind. He had cut out a windowpane to get in. I'm sure of that, because that's what he always does. I think he would do it even if the door was open, because he's a bit of an obsessive, or maybe just superstitious.'

'So he wasn't seen?'

'Yes, he was. When he ran across the garden.'

'He mentioned a garden too?'

'I'm not making this up. I'm saying that as he was running across the garden someone looked out of the window and shone an electric torch on him, probably Alfred's own torch, which he hadn't managed to pick up. He leaped on to his bike and rode off without turning round, right down to the Seine – I don't know where exactly – and threw his bike into the river, in case it would help identify him. He didn't dare come home. He made his way to Gare du Nord on foot and telephoned me and begged me to say nothing. I pleaded with him not to run away. I tried reasoning with him. In the end he promised to write to me poste restante to tell me where he was so that I could join him.'

'Has he written yet?'

'There hasn't been enough time for a letter to arrive. I went to the post office this morning. I've been thinking about it for the last twenty-four hours. I bought all the newspapers, expecting to read a report about a murdered woman.'

Maigret picked up the phone and rang the police station at Neuilly.

'Hello! Police Judiciaire here. Have you had any murder recorded in the last twenty-four hours?'

'Just a moment. I will hand you over to the secretary. I'm just the orderly.'

Maigret made absolutely sure:

'No bodies found on the public highway? No night calls? No bodies fished out of the Seine?'

'Absolutely nothing, sir.'

'No one reported a gunshot?'

'No one.'

La Grande Perche waited patiently, like someone on a social visit, her hands joined and resting on her bag.

'You understand why I came to see you?'

'I think so.'

'At first, I thought that perhaps the police had seen Alfred, in which case his bicycle alone would have given him away. Then there are the tools that he left behind. Now that he's fled over the border no one will believe his story. And . . . he is no safer in Belgium or Holland than he is in Paris. I'd rather see him in prison for attempted burglary, even if it means he goes down for another five years, than to see him accused of murder.'

'The problem is,' said Maigret, 'that there is no corpse.'

'You think he made it up, or that I made it up?'

He didn't reply.

'It will be easy for you to find the house where he did the job that night. Maybe I shouldn't tell you this, but I'm sure you will think of it yourself. It's almost certain the safe is one that he installed himself. Planchart surely have a list of their clients. There can't be many in Neuilly who bought a safe from them at least seventeen years ago.'

'Did Albert have any other girlfriends apart from you?'

17

'Ah! I should have seen that one coming. I'm not the jealous type, and even if I was I wouldn't be telling you lies just to get my revenge, if that's what you're thinking. He doesn't have a girlfriend because he doesn't want one, the poor man. If he did, I'd be able to fix him up with whatever he wanted.'

'Why?'

'Because he doesn't have much fun in his life.'

'Do you have any money?'

'No.'

'What will you do?'

'I'll get by, you know me. I'm only here to tell you that Freddie didn't kill anyone.'

'If he wrote to you, would you show me the letter?'

'You'll read it before me. Now that you know he said he'd write to me poste restante, you'll monitor all the post offices in Paris. You forget that I know how things work.'

She had stood up, very tall; she looked at him, sitting at his desk, from head to toe.

'If everything I've heard about you is true, there is a chance that you will believe me.'

'Why?'

'Because otherwise you'd be a fool. And you aren't. You're going to telephone Planchart.'

'Yes.'

'Will you keep me informed?'

He considered her without replying and realized that, despite himself, there was a smile of amusement playing about his lips.

'Please yourself, then,' she sighed. 'I could be of use to you. No matter how long you've been in this game, there are still things that people like us know better than you.'

This 'us' obviously referred to a whole world of people, the one that La Grande Perche belonged to, living on the other side of the barrier.

'If Inspector Boissier wasn't on holiday, I'm sure he would back up everything I have told you about Alfred.'

'He isn't on holiday. He leaves tomorrow.'

She opened her bag and took out a piece of paper.

'I'll leave you the phone number of the bar downstairs from us. If you ever need to come and see me, I promise you I won't strip off. Nowadays I prefer to keep my dress on!'

There was just a slight hint of bitterness in her voice. But then, a moment later she was poking fun at herself:

'Much better for all concerned!'

It was only after he had closed the door behind her that Maigret realized that he had quite naturally shaken the hand that she had offered to him. The wasp was still buzzing round just below the ceiling, as if looking for a way out, completely oblivious of the wide-open windows. Madame Maigret had said this morning that she would be going to the flower market and asked him, if he was free around midday, to meet her there. It was midday. He hesitated, leaned out of the window, from where he saw the splashes of vivid colours behind the parapet of the embankment.

Then he picked up the phone with a sigh.

'Ask Boissier to come and see me.'

Seventeen years had elapsed since the farcical events of Rue de la Lune, and Maigret was now an important person at the head of the Murder Squad. A funny notion came into his head, an almost childish craving. He lifted the phone again.

'Brasserie Dauphine, please.'

At the exact moment that Boissier was coming through the door, he said:

'Send me up a Pernod, please.'

Then, seeing the inspector with large rings of sweat under the arms of his shirt, he added:

'Make that two. Two Pernods. Thank you.'

Boissier, a true southerner, twitched his blue-black moustache with pleasure and went to sit on the window-sill, where he mopped his brow.

2.

In which we encounter Inspector Boissier, and then a house with a garden and gate in front of it, and hear of a meeting Maigret has in front of this gate

After taking a swig of his Pernod, Maigret launched in:

'Tell me, Boissier, old man, what do you know about Alfred Jussiaume?'

'Sad Freddie?'

'Yes.'

Immediately Boissier's brow darkened, and he cast Maigret a sly glance. Forgetting to sip his drink, he asked in a worried voice:

'Has he done a job?'

It was always like this with him, and Maigret knew why. By treating him with the utmost care, Maigret was the only one who found favour in Boissier's eyes. By rights, Boissier should have advanced much further in the police and would have done years ago but for his inability to spell and his elementary handwriting, which had meant he failed even the most basic exams.

For once, however, the top brass had made the right call. They had appointed Detective Chief Inspector Peuchet, a dozy old buffer, as head of the squad, and, apart from drawing up reports, it was Boissier who did all the work and managed his team.

Their department didn't deal with homicides, as Maigret's did. Nor did they deal with the amateurs, the sales assistants who make off with the takings and other such small fry.

The clients Boissier and his team dealt with were the professionals of the ignoble art of stealing, from the jewel thieves who trawled the big hotels along the Champs-Élysées to the housebreakers and hustlers who, like Jussiaume, hung out in the seedy corners of the city.

Because of this, they had a quite different outlook to the Crime Squad. In Boissier's world, there were professionals on both sides of the divide. Their battle was a battle between specialists. It wasn't a matter of psychology; rather it involved detailed knowledge of all the tics and personal foibles of all their opponents.

It was not unusual to see Inspector Boissier sitting entirely at his ease on a café terrace in the company of a cat burglar. Maigret, for example, would never have had a conversation of this type with a murderer:

'Hey, Julot, you haven't done a job for a while.'

'You're quite right, inspector.'

'When was the last time I hauled you in?'

'It must have been around six months ago.'

'The coffers are a bit empty, then? I'd wager you're planning something.'

The thought of Sad Freddie pulling off a job without him knowing about it rubbed Boissier up the wrong way.

'I don't know if he's been on a job recently, but I've just had La Grande Perche in my office.'

That was enough to reassure Boissier.

'She doesn't know anything,' he confirmed. 'Alfred is not the sort to confide in a woman, not even his own wife.'

The portrait that Boissier painted of Jussiaume was fairly similar to the one Ernestine had presented, except that he placed more emphasis on the man's professionalism.

'I hate it when I have to arrest someone like him and send him down. The last time, when he got five years, I almost felt like giving his lawyer a piece of my mind; he had no idea what to do. He's a waste of space, that one.'

It was hard to define quite what Boissier understood by 'waste of space', but you knew exactly what he meant.

'There's no one in Paris as good as Alfred at getting into an inhabited house and doing it over without making a noise, without even waking the cat. From a technical point of view, he's an artist. What's more, he doesn't need any-one to tip him off, act as lookout or any of that. He works alone and never loses his nerve. He doesn't drink, he doesn't talk, he doesn't go round the bars playing the hard guy. A man of his skills should be rich as Croesus. He knows the exact location and the mechanical specifications of hundreds of safes he has installed himself; you'd think he'd only have to go in there and help himself. But every time he goes for it, something goes wrong, or else he ends up with peanuts.'

Perhaps Boissier was speaking like this because he saw in Sad Freddie an image of his own life, with the difference that he enjoyed an iron constitution that could withstand all the aperitifs drunk on café terraces and the countless nights spent on stakeouts in all weathers.

'The funny thing is, if you put him away for ten, twenty years, he'd still start again the moment he got out, even if he was seventy years old and on crutches. He tells himself he just needs one big payday, just one; he feels he deserves it after all these years.'

'He's had a bad break,' Maigret explained. 'It appears that, on the point of cracking a safe in Neuilly, he noticed that there was a dead body in the room.'

'What did I tell you? It could only happen to him. So he scarpered? What's he done with his bike?'

'Thrown it in the Seine.'

'Is he in Belgium?'

'Probably.'

'I'll telephone Brussels, unless you don't want him found.'

'I very much want him found.'

'Do you know where it happened?'

'I know it was a house in Neuilly, and it has a garden and a gate out front.'

'Easy. I'll be right back.'

While he was away, Maigret had the good grace to order two more Pernods from the Brasserie Dauphine. The smell evoked not only Rue de la Lune but also the Midi, particularly a little bar in Cannes where he had once conducted an investigation, and suddenly the case seemed different from the norm and almost took on the feeling of a holiday jaunt.

He hadn't made a definite arrangement to meet Madame Maigret at the flower market, and she knew him well enough not to wait. Boissier returned with a dossier, from which he produced some identification photos of Alfred Jussiaume.

'That's his face.'

The face of an ascetic, really, rather than a thug. There was hardly any flesh on his bones, his nostrils were long and pinched, and there was something almost mystical in his gaze. Even in these stark mug shots, without a false collar and with his Adam's apple protruding, you could sense the deep loneliness of the man, and a sadness that was in no way aggressive.

Jussiaume had been born to be hunted, and he found it completely normal.

'Would you like me to read you his record?'

'That won't be necessary today. I'd prefer to read it later in my own time. What I would like to see is the list.'

These words pleased Boissier, and Maigret knew it when he said them, because they paid homage to his colleague's professionalism.

'You knew that I'd have it?'

'I was sure that you would.'

Indeed, Boissier did know his trade. The list in question was the one taken from the records of Planchart of all the safes installed during the time of Alfred Jussiaume.

'Let me find Neuilly. You're sure it was Neuilly?'

'That's what Ernestine says.'

'You know, she's no fool coming to see you. But why you?'

'Because I arrested her, sixteen or seventeen years ago, and she played a mean trick on me.'

That came as no surprise to Boissier; it was all part of the game. They both knew how the thing worked. The gently glinting Pernod in their glasses had filled the office with its scent, driving the wasp to new heights of frenzy.

'A bank . . . That can't be it . . . Freddie never does banks, he doesn't like the electrical alarm systems . . . An oil company, but it closed down ten years ago . . . A perfumier . . . went bust last year.'

Finally, Boissier's finger landed on a name and address.

'Guillaume Serre, dentist, 43a, Rue de la Ferme, Neuilly. Do you know it? It's just past the Botanical Garden, runs parallel with Boulevard Richard-Wallace.'

'I know it.'

They looked at each other for a moment.

'Are you busy?' asked Maigret.

And again he knew he was pandering to Boissier's self-esteem.

'I was just doing some paperwork. I'm off to Brittany tomorrow.'

'Shall we go?'

'I'll get my jacket and hat. Shall I ring Brussels first?'

'Yes. Holland too.'

'All right.'

They took the bus there, riding on the rear platform. Rue de la Ferme was a quiet, provincial-looking street; they spotted a small restaurant with four tables out on the terrace, between potted green plants, and sat down to have something to eat.

Inside, there were just three builders in white smocks, having lunch and drinking red wine. Some flies were buzzing round Maigret and Boissier as they waited. Further down the street on the opposite side they saw a black gate that could only belong to number 43a.

They weren't in any hurry. If there really had been a dead body inside the house, the murderer would have had more than twenty-four hours to get rid of it.

A waitress in a black dress and white apron took their orders, but the owner also came out to greet them.

'Good afternoon, gentlemen.'

'Good afternoon. Do you, by any chance, know of a dentist around here?'

A flick of the chin.

'There's one just there across the street, but I don't know what he's like. My wife prefers to get her teeth seen to on Boulevard Sébastopol. I think he's probably quite expensive. People aren't exactly queueing up to see him.'

'Do you know him?'

The owner hesitated and gave them both a long look, especially Boissier.

'Police, eh?'

On balance, Maigret thought it better to say yes.

'Has he done something?'

'We are simply looking for help with our inquiries. What's he like?'

'Taller and stronger than either you or me,' he said, looking at Maigret. 'I weigh ninety-eight kilos; he must weigh around a hundred and five.'

'How old?'

'Fifty, maybe? Around that sort of age. Not that well dressed, which is surprising in a dentist. Looks a bit like a crusty old bachelor.'

'He's not married?'

'Just a minute . . . Now I think about it, he did get married about two years ago . . . There's also an old woman living in the house – his mother, I suppose. She does the shopping every morning . . .'

'Do they have a maid?'

'Just a cleaning lady. To be honest, I'm not very sure. I only know him because he occasionally pops in here on the sly.'

'On the sly?'

'Just a manner of speaking. People like him aren't in the habit of frequenting cafés like this one. When he does come here, he's always casting a glance at the house, as if he's checking that he's not being watched. He always looks very furtive when he orders a drink at the bar.

'"A red wine!" he says. Never anything else. I know not to put the bottle away afterwards, because he always orders a second one. He knocks them back straight, wipes his mouth and has the money already in his hand.'

'Does he ever get drunk?'

'Never. Two glasses, and that's his lot. When he leaves I see him slip a cachou lozenge or a clove into his mouth to take away the smell of the wine.'

'What's his mother like?'

'A wizened old woman, always dressed in black, who never says hello to anyone; she doesn't seem the easy-going type.'

'And the wife?'

'I've only ever spotted her as they drive past in the car, but I've heard she's a foreigner. She's tall and sturdy like him, dark complexion.'

'Do you think they are away on holiday?'

'Hold on. I think the last time I served him his two glasses was two or three days ago.'

'Two or three?'

'Let's think. It was the evening the plumber came to fix the beer pump. I'll check with my wife to make sure I'm not talking nonsense.'

It was the day before yesterday, Tuesday in other words, a few hours before Alfred Jussiaume discovered a woman's body in the house.

'Can you remember what time it was?'

'He usually pops in around six thirty in the evening.'

'Was he on foot?'

'Yes. They do have an old car, but this is when he goes for his evening walk. Can you tell me what all this is about?'

'Nothing, at present. We're trying to establish some facts.'

The man didn't believe him, that much was evident in his face.

'Will you be back?'

Then, turning to the inspector:

'You're not Detective Chief Inspector Maigret, by any chance, are you?'

'Did someone tell you?'

'One of the builders inside thought he recognized you. If it is you, my wife will be very pleased to meet you in the flesh.'

'We'll be back,' he promised.

They had had a good meal and sampled the calvados that the owner, who was from Falaise, had offered them. They were now walking on the pavement on the shady side of the street. Maigret was smoking his pipe with small puffs. Boissier had lit a cigarette; two of the fingertips on his right hand were stained brown by the tobacco like a seasoned old pipe.

It was possible to imagine that you were in a small village more than a hundred kilometres from Paris. There were more private houses than apartment blocks, some of them grand middle-class mansions dating from the eighteenth or nineteenth century.

There was only one gate in the street, a black metal one, behind which lay a lawn that looked like a green carpet in the sunlight. A copper nameplate read:

Guillaume Serre
Dental Surgeon

And in smaller letters underneath:

2 to 5 p.m. and by appointment

The sun beat down on the façade of the house, warming the yellowish stone, and the shutters were closed at all but two of the windows. Boissier could sense Maigret hesitating.

'Are you going over?'

Before crossing the road, he glanced both ways down the street and frowned. Boissier looked in the direction that Maigret was staring.

'La Grande Perche!' he exclaimed.

She was coming down from Boulevard Richard-Wallace and was wearing the same green hat as that morning. When she noticed Maigret and his companion, she came to a halt, then made a beeline for them.

'Are you surprised to see me here?'

'You knew the address?'

'I telephoned your office about half an hour ago. I wanted to tell you that I'd found the list. I knew it was around somewhere. I've seen Alfred consulting it, marking it with crosses. When I left you this morning, I thought of a place where Alfred might have hidden it.'

'Where?'

'Do I have to tell you?'

'It would be better if you did.'

'I'd rather not. Not right now.'

'What else did you find?'

'What makes you think I found something else?'

'You didn't have any money this morning, yet you came here by taxi.'

'That's true. There was some money.'

'A lot?'

'More than I expected.'

'Where is the list?'

'I burned it.'

'Why?'

'Because of the crosses. They probably refer to addresses Alfred has burgled, and I won't go as far as providing you with evidence against him.'

She glanced at the front of the house.

'Are you going in?'

Maigret nodded.

'Would it bother you if I waited for you on the terrace over there?'

She hadn't said a word to Boissier, who was giving her a stern look.

'If you wish,' said Maigret.

And, accompanied by his colleague, he stepped out of the shadow into the sunlight, while Ernestine's tall silhouette headed off to the terrace.

It was ten past two. If the dentist wasn't away on holiday he should, according to his nameplate, be in his surgery ready to receive patients. There was an electric button to the right of the gateway; Maigret pressed it, and the gate opened automatically. He walked across the small garden and found another button at the front door of the house, which did not open automatically. After the bell had rung inside there was a long silence. The two men strained to hear, both sure they could sense a presence on the other side of the panel, and looked at each other. Finally, a chain was pulled back, the latch was released, and the door opened a small crack.

'Do you have an appointment?'

'We wish to speak to Dr Serre.'

'He only sees patients by appointment.'

The door did not open any wider. They could just make out, behind the door, the silhouette and the thin face of an old woman.

'According to your sign—'

'That sign is twenty-five years old.'

'Would you be so kind as to tell your son that Detective Chief Inspector Maigret would like to see him?'

The door didn't move for a moment or two, then it opened to reveal a wide corridor with a black-and-white tiled floor reminiscent of the corridor in a convent. The old woman who ushered them in would not have looked out of place dressed in a nun's habit.

'You must forgive me, detective chief inspector, but my son does not care to take patients off the street.'

The woman wasn't bad looking. She had a surprising elegance and dignity about her. She was smiling to try to wipe away the bad first impression she had made.

'Please, do come in. I will have to ask you to wait a short while. For the last few years my son has been taking an afternoon nap, especially in the summer, and he is still in bed. If you would care to come this way . . .'

She led them through some varnished oak double doors to the left, and Maigret had an even stronger feeling of being in a convent, or rather, a well-to-do priest's house. The smell in particular – faint and mysterious – reminded him of something; he couldn't think what and strained to remember. The living room they entered into was illuminated only by the light coming through the slats of the shutters; after the heat of the outside, it felt refreshingly cool.

The sounds of the city didn't seem to be able to penetrate all the way in, and you got the impression that nothing had changed in this house for more than a century, that the upholstered armchairs, side tables, piano and china figurines had always stood in the same place. Even the enlarged photographs in black wooden frames hanging on the wall looked as if they had been taken in the era of Nadar. There was a man in a restrictive collar from an earlier century with large bushy sideburns, and, on the facing wall, a woman of about forty, a parting in her hair, who bore a resemblance to Empress Eugénie.

The old lady herself could almost have appeared in one of these portraits. She continued to attend to them, showing them to their chairs, her hands joined in a solicitous gesture.

'I don't wish to pry, detective chief inspector, but my son has no secrets from me. We have never been apart, even though he is now in his fifties. I have no idea of the purpose of your visit, so before I wake him I would like to know . . .'

Leaving that sentence hanging, she beamed a benevolent smile in their direction.

'Your son is married, I believe?'

'He has been married twice.'

'Is his second wife here?'

There was a hint of sadness in her eyes. Boissier started crossing and uncrossing his legs: this wasn't the sort of milieu he felt comfortable in.

'She isn't here any more, inspector.'

She walked softly to the door and closed it. She returned and took a seat on the corner of a sofa, sitting bolt upright, as young girls are taught to do in convent schools.

'I hope she hasn't done anything silly,' she said in a low voice. 'If you're here about her I will need to ask you some questions before I wake my son. Is it because of her that you have come?'

Did Maigret give a slight nod to this question? He wasn't sure himself. He was far too fascinated by the atmosphere of this house and even more so by this woman: behind the gentle exterior there was a formidable energy at work.

She didn't strike a single false note: neither in her dress, nor in her bearing, nor in her voice. She was someone you might have expected to come across in a chateau or rather in one of those sprawling country houses that are like museums of a bygone age.

'When he was widowed fifteen years ago my son did not consider remarrying for a long time.'

'But he did remarry – two years ago, if I am not mistaken?'

She displayed no surprise that he was so well informed.

'Indeed. Two and a half years to be exact. He married one of his patients, a woman of a certain age, like himself. She was forty-seven at the time. Originally from Holland, she was living on her own in Paris. I won't live for ever, inspector. I sit before you now, a woman of seventy-six.'

'You don't look it.'

'I know. My mother lived to the age of ninety-two, and my grandmother died in an accident at the age of eighty-eight.'

'And your father?'

'He died young.'

She said this as if it were of no importance, or rather, as if it was in the nature of things for men to die young.

'I almost encouraged Guillaume to remarry; I told myself that that way he wouldn't end up on his own.'

'Was the marriage an unhappy one?'

'Not exactly unhappy. Not at the beginning. I believe all the problems came from her being a foreigner. There are all sorts of little things that you can't adapt to. I don't know how to describe it to you . . . Just things to do with food, liking some dishes but not others. Also, perhaps, when she married my son she thought he was richer than he actually is.'

'She had no fortune herself?'

'A certain amount. She wasn't penniless, but with the rise in the cost of living . . .'

'When did she die?'

The old woman looked at him with wide eyes.

'Die?'

'I'm sorry, I thought she was dead. You speak about her in the past tense.'

She smiled.

'That's true, but not for the reason you imagine. She's not dead, though to us it feels that way. She left.'

'After an argument?'

'Guillaume is not the sort of man who has arguments.'

'With you?'

'I'm too old to have arguments any more, inspector. I've seen it all before. I know all about life and I let people—'

36

'When did she leave the house?'

'Two days ago.'

'Did she tell you she was leaving?'

'My son and I both knew she would leave sooner or later.'

'Has she spoken to you about it?'

'Often.'

'Did she give a reason?'

She didn't reply immediately, seemed to be thinking.

'Would you like me to tell you what I really think? If I sound a bit hesitant, it is because I am worried that you will make fun of me. I don't like talking about such matters in front of men but I suppose a police inspector is like a doctor or a priest.'

'Are you a Catholic, Madame Serre?'

'Yes. My daughter-in-law was a Protestant. Not that that matters. You see, she was at that difficult age for a woman. All we women, more or less, go through this period of a few years when we are not ourselves. We get irritated by the most trivial things. We can so easily get the wrong end of the stick.'

'I understand. And that was what was going on here?'

'That and other things besides, probably. By the end she was thinking about nothing but her native Holland; she spent days writing to the friends she had kept in touch with back there.'

'Did your son ever go to Holland with her?'

'Never.'

'So she left on Tuesday?'

'She took the nine-forty train from Gare du Nord.'

'The night train?'

'Yes. She had spent all day packing her bags.'

'Did your son accompany her to the station?'

'No.'

'Did she call a taxi?'

'She went out to hail one at the corner of Boulevard Richard-Wallace.'

'Have you had any word from her since?'

'No. I don't think she feels the need to write to us.'

'Was divorce ever discussed?'

'I told you we are Catholics. Besides, my son has no desire to remarry. I still don't understand what on earth can have brought about this visit by the police.'

'I would like to ask you, madame, to describe exactly what happened in the house on Tuesday evening. One moment. You have a maid, don't you?'

'No, inspector. Our cleaning lady, Eugénie, comes every morning at nine o'clock and stays until five.'

'Is she here today?'

'You have come on her day off. She will be here tomorrow.'

'Does she live in the neighbourhood?'

'She lives in Puteaux, on the other side of the Seine. Just above a hardware shop opposite the bridge.'

'I assume she helped your daughter-in-law to pack her bags?'

'She brought the bags downstairs.'

'How many suitcases?'

'To be precise, one trunk and two leather suitcases. There was also a jewellery case and a toilet bag.'

'Did Eugénie leave at five o'clock as normal?'

'Indeed she did. Forgive me if I look a little put out. I have never been questioned in this manner before and I confess I—'

'Did your son go out that evening?'

'What do you mean by "evening"?'

'Let's say, just before dinner.'

'He went for a walk, as usual.'

'Presumably to drink an aperitif?'

'He doesn't drink.'

'Never?'

'Just a glass of wine mixed with water at each meal. Certainly not those terrible drinks they call aperitifs.'

Boissier, who had been sitting quietly in his armchair, seemed at that moment to inhale the last trace of aniseed clinging to his moustache.

'We sat down for dinner as soon as he got back. He always follows the same route. He got into the habit when we used to have a dog and he took it for walks at the same time each day. Now he carries on the same routine.'

'You don't have a dog any more?'

'Not for four years, since Bibi died.'

'No cat?'

'My daughter-in-law hated cats. You see? I'm talking about her in the past tense because we now consider that period of our lives to be over.'

'Did all three of you sit down to dinner?'

'Maria came down as I was serving the soup.'

'Did you talk about anything?'

'Not a thing. The meal took place in silence. I knew that, in spite of everything, Guillaume was quite upset. He comes across as a cold fish, but in fact he is a highly sensitive boy. And when you have been on such intimate terms with someone for more than two years . . .'

Maigret and Boissier had not heard a thing, but the old lady had sharper hearing. She leaned her head as if listening. It was a mistake, because Maigret realized what the sound was and got up to open the door. There was a man, taller, broader and heavier than the inspector, looking rather shamefaced, who had clearly been listening outside the door for some time.

His mother had not been lying when she had said he was taking a nap. His sparse hair was messed up and plastered to his forehead, and he had pulled some trousers on over his white shirt, which was unbuttoned at the collar. He was wearing carpet slippers.

'Come in, Monsieur Serre,' said Maigret.

'I beg your pardon. I heard some sounds. I thought . . .'

He talked deliberately, turning his heavy, slow gaze on each of them in turn.

'These gentlemen are from the police,' his mother explained as she stood up.

He didn't ask any questions, merely looked at them again and buttoned up his shirt.

'Madame Serre was telling us that your wife left you the day before yesterday.'

This time it was the old woman he looked at, with a frown. His large body was flabby, like his face, but unlike a lot of big men he did not give an impression of lightness.

His skin was pale and lustreless; he had tufts of hair sprouting from his nose and ears, and his eyebrows were exceptionally bushy.

'What do these gentlemen want exactly?' he asked, enunciating each syllable distinctly.

'I don't know.'

And Maigret was at something of a loss. Boissier, for his part, wondered how the inspector was going to deal with this. These weren't the sort of people you could give the third degree.

'As it happens, Monsieur Serre, your wife merely cropped up in the conversation. Your mother told us you were having a nap, and we were just chatting idly while we waited for you. We're here, my colleague and I' (and Boissier derived great pleasure from hearing that word 'colleague') 'because we have reason to believe that you were the victim of an attempted burglary.'

Serre was not a man to break eye contact. On the contrary, he stared at Maigret as if trying to see his innermost thoughts.

'What gave you that idea?'

'We received a tip-off.'

'I presume you are referring to police informers.'

'If you like.'

'I'm sorry, gentlemen.'

'You weren't burgled?'

'If I had been, I would not have hesitated to inform the police myself.'

He was making no attempt to be friendly. Not the faintest trace of a smile passed his lips.

'Do you own a safe?'

'I believe I have a right not to reply. However, I don't see any reason not to tell you that I have one.'

His mother was trying to signal to him, presumably to advise him not to be so truculent.

He got the message but didn't change his tone.

'Unless I am mistaken it is a Planchart safe, installed eighteen years ago.'

He didn't show any reaction, He remained standing while Maigret and Boissier sat in the semi-darkness, and Maigret noticed that he had the same broad chin as the man in the portrait, and the same eyebrows. Whimsically, Maigret imagined what he would look like with sideburns.

'I don't recall when it was installed, not that it is anyone's business but mine.'

'When we came in I noticed that the front door is fitted with a security lock and a chain.'

'Lots of doors are.'

'Do you sleep on the first floor, you and your mother?'

Serre pointedly refused to answer.

'Are your study and your surgery on the ground floor?'

From the old woman's movements, Maigret understood that they were the two rooms that led on from the living room.

'Do I have your permission to take a look?'

He hesitated, opened his mouth, and Maigret felt sure he was going to say no. His mother sensed this too and pre-empted him.

'Why not allow the gentlemen to do as they ask? They will be able to see for themselves that there wasn't any break-in.'

The man shrugged his shoulders, still looking stubborn and sullen, and he elected not to follow them into the neighbouring rooms.

Madame Serre took them first into the study, which was as hushed and old-fashioned-looking as the living room. Behind a black leather chair there was a large safe painted dark green, of a rather old design. Boissier went up to it and examined its metal exterior with his hand.

'As you see, everything is in order,' said the old woman. 'You mustn't mind my son's bad mood, but . . .'

She fell silent as she noticed her son standing in the doorway, still glaring at them.

Then, indicating the bound books that lined the shelves in the room, she tried to lighten the mood.

'Don't be surprised to see all these law books here. They belonged to my husband, who was a lawyer.'

She opened a final door. The décor here was more familiar: it looked like any standard dentist's surgery, with its reclining chair and the usual range of instruments. The lower halves of the windowpanes were frosted. As they returned to the study, Boissier went over to one of the windows, ran his fingers over it and tipped Maigret the nod.

'Was this pane replaced recently?' Maigret asked.

The old woman replied without hesitation:

'Four days ago. The window was left open during that big storm that you no doubt remember.'

'Did you call in a glazier?'

'No.'

'Who replaced the glass?'

'My son. He likes doing odd jobs. He is always fixing things around the house.'

Then Guillaume Serre spoke up with a note of impatience.

'These gentlemen have no right to be pestering us, Mother. Don't answer any more questions.'

She turned her back on him and gave Maigret a smile that seemed to say:

'Don't pay any attention. I did warn you.'

She saw them out as far as the front door, while her son stayed in the middle of the living room. Leaning over, she whispered:

'If you need to talk to me, come back when he is not here.'

They found themselves back out in the sunshine, which immediately made their clothes stick to them. Once outside the gate – even the way it squeaked evoked a convent – they spotted the green hat of Ernestine, who was sitting on the terrace of the bistro on the other side of the street.

Maigret hesitated. He could easily have turned left and avoided her altogether. It almost felt as if they were going across to her to give her a report.

Perhaps out of embarrassment, Maigret muttered:

'Shall we have a beer?'

Ernestine watched them approach with a questioning look.

3.

Where Ernestine covers her modesty with a dressing gown, and the old woman from Neuilly pays Maigret a visit

'What did you do today?' asked Madame Maigret, as they sat down to eat next to the open window.

In the houses opposite they could see other people having dinner, identical splashes of white where the men had taken off their jackets and were in shirt-sleeves. Some had already eaten and were leaning out of their windows. There was a sound of music on the radio, babies crying, raised voices. One or two concierges had brought a chair to sit outside their main entrance doors.

'Nothing out of the ordinary,' Maigret replied. 'Possible homicide of a Dutch woman, who may in fact be alive and well somewhere.'

It was too soon to go into detail. In fact, everything had proceeded at a slow pace. They had lingered a long time on the little terrace on Rue de la Ferme, Boissier, Ernestine and him, and, of the three of them, Ernestine had been the most excited.

She said indignantly:

'Is he making out it isn't true?'

The owner brought them some beers.

'Actually, he didn't say anything. His mother did all the talking. He did little more than see us off the premises.'

'He claims that there was no dead body in the study?'

She had evidently got some information from the wine merchant on the inhabitants of the house behind the gate.

'So why did he not inform the police that his house had been broken into?'

'According to him there was no break-in.'

Clearly familiar with Sad Freddie's methods, she said:

'Is there a pane of glass missing from the window?'

Boissier gave Maigret a look as if to tell him to stay silent, but the inspector ignored it.

'A pane has been recently replaced. It appears it was broken four or five days ago, on the night of the storm.'

'He's lying.'

'Someone is lying, for sure.'

'You think it's me?'

'I didn't say that. It could be Alfred.'

'Why would he have told me all this over the telephone?'

'Perhaps he didn't,' Boissier interjected, watching her closely.

'Why would I have made it up? Do you think that too?' she said, turning to Maigret.

'I don't think anything.'

He smiled vaguely. He felt good, mellow even. The beer was cool, and the shade had a flavour to it, like in the country, perhaps because the Bois de Boulogne was so close by.

A lazy afternoon. They had drunk two beers. Then, rather than leave the girl on her own in the centre of Paris, they had taken her in a taxi and dropped her off at Châtelet.

'Give me a ring as soon as you receive a letter.'

He could sense that she was disappointed in him, that she had imagined him differently. She was probably saying to herself that he had got old, had become just like the others and was only half-heartedly pursuing the case.

'Shall I postpone my holiday?' Boissier had asked him.

'I assume your wife is packing your bags?'

'They're already at the station. We're due to take the six o'clock train tomorrow morning.'

'With your daughter?'

'Of course.'

'Then go.'

'Won't you need my help?'

'You've given me the file already.'

Once he was on his own in his office, he almost had a nap in his chair. The wasp had gone. The sun had passed over to the other side of the embankment. Lucas had been on holiday since midday. He called Janvier, who had already taken his holiday back in June, to attend a family wedding.

'Sit down. I have a job for you. Have you finished your report?'

'I've just completed it.'

'Good. Now, write this down. First I want you to go to the town hall in Neuilly and find the maiden name of a Dutch woman who, two years ago, married one Guillaume Serre, resident at 43a, Rue de la Ferme.'

'Easy.'

'Probably. She must have been living in Paris for some time. Try to find out where, what she did, who her family are, how well off she was, etc.'

'Got it, chief.'

'She's supposed to have left the house on Rue de la Ferme between eight and nine o'clock on Tuesday evening, intending to take the night train to Holland. She allegedly hailed a taxi herself at the corner of Boulevard Richard-Wallace to take her and her luggage to the station.'

Janvier was writing columns of notes in his notebook.

'Is that all?'

'No. Get some men to help you, to save time. I want you to question the people in the neighbourhood, trades-men, etc., about the Serres.'

'How many are there?'

'A mother and her son. The mother is nearly eighty and the son is a dentist. Try to locate the taxi. Question the station and train staff too.'

'Can I use one of the cars?'

'You can.'

As for Maigret, that is more or less all he did that afternoon. He had got in touch with the Belgian police, who had received the alert about Sad Freddie but hadn't found him yet. He had also had a long conversation with the inspector in charge of passport control at Jeumont, on the Belgian border. The latter had personally inspected the train that Alfred would have travelled on and could not recollect seeing anyone matching the safe-cracker's description.

That didn't mean anything. He would just have to wait. Maigret signed off a few forms in the absence of the commissioner, went for an aperitif at the Brasserie Dauphine with his colleague from Special Branch, then took the bus home.

'What shall we do?' asked Madame Maigret once she had cleared the table.

'Let's go for a walk.'

In other words, they would take a stroll down to the Grands Boulevards and end up sitting on a café terrace. The sun had set. The air had grown cooler, but there was still the occasional warm gust that seemed to rise from the pavement. The bar front had been opened up, and a depleted band was playing some music inside. Like them, most of the customers sat at their tables without a word, watching the world go by, their faces becoming more and more obscured by the dusk. Later the electric lights came on and revealed them in a new aspect. Like the other couples, Maigret and his wife ambled home, her hand in the crook of his arm.

Then a new morning, the sun as bright as the day before.

Instead of heading straight to the Police Judiciaire, Maigret made a detour via Quai de Jemmapes, recognized the green-painted bistro, next to the Saint-Martin Lock, with the words 'Snacks served all day' on the front, and went up to the bar.

'A white wine.'

Then he asked the question. The man from Auvergne serving behind the bar answered directly.

'I can't tell you exactly what time it was, but there was a telephone call. It was daytime already. Neither my wife nor I had got up, because at that time of the morning it couldn't possibly be for us. Ernestine came down. I heard her have a long conversation.'

That was one thing, at least, that wasn't a lie.

'What time did Alfred leave the previous evening?'

'Maybe eleven o'clock? Maybe earlier? One thing I remember was that he took his bike.'

A door from the bar gave directly on to a corridor, and from there a staircase led to the floor above. The wall of the staircase was whitewashed, as in the country. They could hear the racket of a crane discharging some sand from a barge a short distance away.

Maigret knocked at another door, which opened. Ernestine appeared in her slip and simply said:

'Oh, it's you.'

Then she went straight to the unmade bed, picked up a dressing gown and slipped it on.

Was that a smile on Maigret's face as he remembered the Ernestine of all those years ago?

'It's an act of charity,' she explained. 'I'm no oil painting these days.'

The window was open. There was a deep-red potted geranium on the sill. The cover of the bed was red too. Through an open door there was a little kitchen, from which emanated a delicious aroma of coffee.

He didn't really know why he had come here.

'Was there anything at the poste restante yesterday evening?'

She looked a little concerned as she replied:

'Nothing.'

'Don't you think it's odd that he hasn't written?'

'Maybe he's suspicious. He must be surprised that there has been nothing in the papers. He probably thinks I'm under surveillance. I was about to pop down to the post office.'

There was an old trunk in the corner.

'Are they his things?'

'His and mine. We don't have that much between us.'

Then, giving him a meaningful look:

'Do you want to look round? Of course you do! I understand. You have to do it. You will find some tools, as he has a spare set, as well as two old suits, a few dresses and some linen.'

As she spoke she emptied the trunk on to the floor and opened all the drawers of a chest.

'I've thought about what you said yesterday. I understand – someone must be lying. It's either those people, the mother and her son, or it's Alfred, or it's me. You have no more reason to believe us than the others.'

'Does Alfred have any family in the country?'

'He has no family anywhere. He only ever had his mother, and she died twenty years ago.'

'Did you ever go anywhere together outside of Paris?'

'No further than Corbeil.'

He wouldn't have sought refuge in Corbeil. It was too close. Maigret was starting to believe that he hadn't gone to Belgium either.

'Is there any place he spoke about, anywhere he wanted to visit one day?'

'He used to talk about the country but wasn't very specific. That meant the world to him.'

'Were you born in the country?'

'Near Nevers, in a hamlet called Saint-Martin-des-Prés.'

She took a postcard from a drawer; it showed the village church with a pond opposite that served as a drinking hole for cattle.

'Did you show him this?'

She caught his drift. Girls like Ernestine cotton on fast.

'I'd be surprised if he went there. He really was near Gare du Nord when he telephoned.'

'How do you know that?'

'I found the bar last night. It's in Rue de Maubeuge, next to a shop selling suitcases. It's called the Bar du Levant. The owner remembered him because he was his first customer of the day. He'd just turned on the coffee maker when Alfred showed up. Would you like a cup of coffee?'

He didn't like to say no, but he had just drunk a glass of white wine.

'No offence.'

After some difficulty finding a taxi, he headed for the Bar du Levant.

'A skinny little guy, sad-looking, eyes red as if he'd been crying' was what he was told.

It was certainly Alfred Jussiaume, whose eyes were often red-rimmed.

'He was speaking on the telephone for a long time. He drank two coffees without sugar and then headed for the station, looking around him, as if he was worried he was being followed. What's he done?'

It was ten o'clock before Maigret climbed the stairs at the Police Judiciaire, where the sun illuminated what seemed like a fog of dust. Contrary to his normal habit, he didn't glance sideways through the windows of the waiting room but went through the inspectors' room, which was almost empty.

'Is Janvier here yet?'

'He came in about eight then went again. He's left a note on your desk.

The note read:

The woman's name is Maria Van Aerts. She is fifty years old and comes from Sneek in Friesland. I'm on my way to Neuilly, where she lived in a family boarding house on Rue de Longchamp. Haven't found the taxi yet. Vacher's checking out the station.

Joseph, the office clerk, opened the door.

'I didn't see you come in, Monsieur Maigret. There is a woman who has been waiting for you for half an hour.'

He handed him a piece of paper, on which old Madame Serre had written her name in her tiny, spidery handwriting.

'Shall I bring her in?'

Maigret put on the jacket he had just removed, went to open the window, filled a pipe and sat down.

'Show her in, yes.'

He wondered what she would be like away from her familiar domestic setting. To his surprise, she didn't look out of place at all. She wasn't dressed in black, as on the

53

previous evening; she was wearing a white dress with a dark printed pattern and a sensible hat. She came towards him with a measured step.

'I think you might have been half-expecting my visit, inspector?'

He hadn't, in fact, but didn't tell her so.

'Sit down, madame.'

'Thank you.'

'Does the smoke bother you?'

'My son smokes cigars all day long. I was so upset yesterday by the way he treated you! I tried to signal to you not to persist, because I know what he's like.'

She showed no signs of nervousness and spoke slowly and deliberately, now and then giving Maigret what appeared to be a conspiratorial smile.

'I think I must have brought him up badly. You see, he is my only child, and he was just seventeen when my husband died. I spoiled him. Guillaume was the only man in the house. If you have children . . .'

Maigret looked at her and tried to figure her out, but didn't manage it. For some reason he then asked:

'Were you born in Paris?'

'In the house you visited yesterday.'

It was a coincidence to find two people in the same inquiry who were born in Paris. Almost always, the people he had dealings with had some sort of connection with the provinces.

'And your husband?'

'His father was also a lawyer, based in Rue de Tocqueville in the seventeenth arrondissement.'

That made three! All this despite the distinctly provincial ambience of the house in Rue de la Ferme.

'It has almost always been just the two of us, my son and me. I guess that is what has made him somewhat unsociable.'

'I thought he had been married once before.'

'He was. His wife didn't live long.'

'How long was it after they were married that she died?'

She opened her mouth to speak. He could see that a sudden thought made her hesitate. He even thought he could see a hint of red rising to her cheeks.

'Two years,' she said finally. 'Odd, isn't it? It has only just struck me. He was with Maria two years too.'

'Who was his first wife?'

'A girl from an excellent family, Jeanne Devoisin, whom we met one summer in Dieppe. We used to go there every year in those days.'

'Was she younger than him?'

'Let's see. He was thirty-two. She was more or less the same age. She was a widow.'

'Did she have any children?'

'No. I didn't know of any family, other than a sister living in Indochina.'

'What did she die of?'

'A heart attack. She had a weak heart and seemed to spend half her life visiting doctors.'

She smiled again.

'I haven't yet told you why I came here. I almost rang you yesterday, when my son was out on his daily walk, then I thought that it would be more proper to come and see you in person. I really must apologize for Guillaume's behaviour towards you and to assure you that it is nothing personal. He can be very anti-social.'

'I noticed.'

'Just the mere thought that you might be suspecting him of having done something wrong . . . He was like this even as a child . . .'

'He lied to me.'

'I beg your pardon?'

The old woman's face displayed genuine shock.

'Why would he lie to you? I don't understand. It's not as if you asked any questions. And it is precisely to respond to those that you wished to ask yesterday that I have come to see you. We have nothing to hide. I don't know what chain of events has led you to our door. It must be some misunderstanding, or a neighbour with a grudge.'

'When was the windowpane broken?'

'I told you, or my son told you, I can't quite remember: the night of the storm last week. I was upstairs and hadn't had time to close all the windows when I heard the crash of breaking glass.'

'Was it still light?'

'It must have been around six in the evening.'

'So your cleaning lady, Eugénie, was no longer in the house?'

'She leaves at five; I thought I had told you that. I didn't tell my son that I was coming to see you. I thought that you would like to visit the house, and it would be a lot easier without him around.'

'You mean during his evening walk?'

'Yes. You will see that we have nothing to hide. We could have cleared everything up yesterday, but for Guillaume's attitude.'

'For the record, Madame Serre, it was you who decided to come here.'

'Of course.'

'And it was you who requested me to ask you some questions.'

She nodded her head.

'So we will begin with the final meal that you had together, you, your son and your daughter-in-law. Your daughter-in-law's bags were already packed. Where in the house were they?'

'In the hallway.'

'Who carried them downstairs?'

'Eugénie carried the cases, and my son took the trunk, which was too heavy for her.'

'Is it a very big trunk?'

'It's what they call a wardrobe trunk. Before they were married, Maria travelled a lot. She has lived in Italy and Egypt.'

'What did you have to eat?'

The question seemed to amuse her and take her by surprise.

'Let me see. I take care of the meals; I will remember. Vegetable soup to start. We always have a vegetable soup, it's healthy. Then we had grilled mackerel and potato purée.'

'For dessert?'

'Chocolate mousse. Yes. My son has always adored chocolate mousse.'

'And you didn't discuss anything at the dinner table? What time did the meal finish?'

'About seven thirty. I put the dishes in the sink and went upstairs.'

'So you weren't there when your daughter-in-law left?'

'I didn't really want to be there. I knew it would be painful and I prefer to avoid emotional scenes. I said goodbye to her in the living room downstairs. I don't resent her. Everyone is different and—'

'Where was your son during this time?'

'In his study, I believe.'

'Do you know whether he had a farewell conversation with his wife?'

'It's unlikely. She came back upstairs. I heard her in her bedroom getting ready.'

'Your house is solidly built, like most old houses. I would guess that, when you are upstairs, it is difficult to hear any sounds from downstairs.'

'Not for me,' she said with a pout.

'What do you mean by that?'

'I have acute hearing. If a floorboard creaks in any room I will hear it.'

'Who went to fetch a taxi?'

'Maria, I told you yesterday.'

'Was she outside long?'

'Quite a long time. There aren't any railway stations nearby, so you have to hope to catch a passing cab.'

'Did you go to the window?'

A slight hesitation.

'Yes.'

'Who carried the trunk to the taxi?'
'The driver.'
'Do you know which company the taxi belonged to?'
'How would I know?'
'What colour was it?'
'A reddish brown, with a crest on the door.'
'Do you remember the driver?'
'Not really. He was short and somewhat fat.'
'How was your daughter-in-law dressed?'
'She was wearing a mauve dress.'
'No coat?'
'She was carrying it over her arm.'
'Was your son still in his study?'
'Yes.'
'What happened next? Did you come downstairs?'
'No.'
'You didn't go to your son?'
'It was he who came upstairs.'
'Straight away?'
'A short while after the taxi left.'
'Was he upset?'
'He was as you found him. He is of a sombre disposition. I have explained to you that he is in fact sensitive and easily affected by the smallest thing.'
'Did he know that his wife wasn't coming back?'
'He guessed that was the case.'
'Had she told him so?'
'Not exactly. She had let it be understood. She talked about needing a change, to see her own country again. Once there, you see . . .'

'What did you do next?'

'I arranged my hair for bed.'

'Was your son with you in your room?'

'Yes.'

'He didn't leave the house?'

'No. Why?'

'Where does he park his car?'

'A hundred metres down the street – some former stables have been converted into private garages. Guillaume rents one of the garages.'

'Is he able to take his car out and put it back without being seen?'

'Why would he want to hide?'

'Did he go back downstairs?'

'I don't know. I think so. I go to bed early, and he tends to stay up reading until eleven o'clock or midnight.'

'In his study?'

'Or in his bedroom.'

'Is his bedroom near yours?'

'Next to mine. We have a bathroom between us.'

'Did you hear him go to bed?'

'I did.'

'At what time?'

'I didn't turn on the light to check.'

'Did you hear any noise later?'

'No.'

'I presume you are always first to come down in the morning?'

'In summer I get up at six thirty.'

'Did you look round all the rooms?'

'I went to the kitchen first of all to put some water on to boil, then I opened the windows, because the air is still cool at that time of day.'

'So you went into the study?'

'Probably.'

'You don't remember?'

'Almost certainly.'

'The broken pane had already been replaced?'

'I think so . . . yes . . .'

'You didn't notice whether anything had been disturbed in the room?'

'Nothing, just the cigar ends in the ashtray, as usual, maybe a book or two not put back on the shelves. I don't know what this is about, inspector. As you see, I am giving honest answers to your questions. I came here with that express purpose.'

'Because you're worried?'

'No. Because I was concerned by the way in which Guillaume received you yesterday. And also because there was something mysterious about your visit. Women aren't like men. When my husband was alive, for example, if there was a noise at night he wouldn't stir from his bed, and it was I who went to have a look. Do you follow? It's probably the same with your wife. Basically, I'm here for more or less the same reason. You spoke about a burglary. You seemed very interested in the subject of Maria.'

'Have you received any news from her?'

'I'm not expecting to hear from her. You are hiding certain facts, and that intrigues me. As when I hear a noise at night, I am telling myself that there is no mystery, that you just have to look at things squarely to establish the simple truth.'

She looked at him, very sure of herself, and Maigret had the feeling that she saw him as a child, like another Guillaume. She seemed to be saying:

'Tell me your concerns. Don't be afraid. You'll see that everything will sort itself out.'

He stared her straight in the face too.

'A man broke into your house that night.'

Her eyes widened in incredulity, with a hint of pity, as if he had said that he believed in werewolves.

'To do what?'

'To burgle your safe.'

'Did he succeed?'

'He got into the house by cutting out a pane of glass in order to open the window.'

'The pane that had been damaged in the storm? Presumably he replaced it afterwards?'

She was still refusing to take what he said seriously.

'What did he steal?'

'He didn't steal anything, because his electric torch revealed an object that he wasn't expecting to find in the room.'

She smiled.

'What object?'

'The body of a middle-aged woman, which may well have been that of your daughter-in-law.'

'He told you that?'

He looked at her hands in their white gloves. They were not trembling.

'Why don't you ask this man to come and repeat these accusations in front of me?'

'He isn't in Paris.'

'Can't you make him come?'

Maigret decided not to reply. He wasn't too pleased with himself. He was beginning to wonder whether he too was succumbing to the influence of this woman, who was as serene and protective as a mother superior.

She didn't stand up, didn't get excited, didn't get angry.

'I don't know what this is about and I won't ask you to explain. No doubt you have your reasons for believing this man. He's a burglar, you say? Whereas I am but an old woman of seventy-six who has never hurt a fly.

'Permit me, now that I am in possession of this information, to invite you to return with me forthwith. I will open all our doors to you, show you anything you wish to see. And my son, once he has been put in the picture, will, I am sure, reply to all your questions too.

'When will you come, Monsieur Maigret?'

This time she was on her feet, still completely at ease. There was no trace of aggression in her manner, perhaps the merest hint of hurt.

'Maybe this afternoon. I'm not sure yet. Has your son used the car these past few days?'

'Ask him yourself, if you would be so kind.'

'Is he at home at the moment?'

'Probably. He was there when I left.'

'Eugénie too?'

'I'm sure she is.'

'Thank you.'

He showed her to the door. Just before leaving, she turned and said in a quiet voice:

'I will ask you one favour. When I leave, please try to put yourself in my place for a moment, and try to forget that you have been dealing with criminals all your life. Imagine that someone has asked you all these questions that you have just put to me; imagine it is you who are suspected of having killed someone in cold blood.'

That was it. She simply added:

'Until this afternoon, Monsieur Maigret.'

The door closed. He stood motionless next to the mantelpiece for a moment or two. Then he went to look out of the window and soon spotted the old woman walking with tiny steps in the bright sunlight in the direction of Pont Saint-Michel.

He picked up the phone.

'Put me through to the police station at Neuilly.'

He was put through, not to the detective chief inspector, but to a junior inspector he knew.

'Vanneau? Maigret here. I'm well, thank you. Listen, this is a delicate matter. Hop in a car and get down to 43a, Rue de la Ferme.'

'The dentist's house? Janvier mentioned it when he was here yesterday. It's about a Dutch woman, is that right?'

'That's not important. Time is short. He's a tricky customer, and I don't want to ask for a warrant just yet. I need you to act quickly, before his mother gets home.'

'Is she far off?'

'At Pont Saint-Michel. She'll probably take a taxi.'

'What should I do with the man?'

'Take him in on some pretext or other. Tell him whatever you like, that you need a witness statement . . .'

'Then what?'

'I'll be there. I just need to go down and get a car.'

'And if the dentist isn't at home?'

'Watch and wait then grab him before he goes back inside the house.'

'Not exactly legal, then?'

'Not in the slightest.'

As Vanneau was about to hang up, he added:

'Take a man with you and post him outside the stables converted into garages further down the street. The dentist rents one of the garages.'

'Got it.'

A moment later Maigret ran downstairs and picked out one of the police cars that were parked in the courtyard. As he turned out in the direction of Pont Neuf, he thought he caught a glimpse of Ernestine in her green hat. He couldn't be sure and didn't want to waste any time. If truth be told, he felt a certain resentment towards La Grande Perche.

Once he had reached Pont Neuf, he repented, but it was too late.

Too bad, she would just have to wait for him.

4.

Where Maigret finds that all interrogations are not the same, and where Eugénie's opinions do not prevent him reaching a categorical conclusion

The police station was situated on the ground floor of the town hall, an ugly square building that stood in the middle of a road junction, surrounded by some scrubby trees and with a dirty flag hanging from the upper storey. Maigret could have gone directly to the inspectors' offices from the front door; instead, to avoid bumping into Guillaume Serre, he made a detour through some draughty corridors and quickly got lost.

Here too there was a feeling of summer relaxation. Doors and windows were wide open, papers fluttered on desks in deserted offices while officers stood around elsewhere in shirt-sleeves, swapping stories about the beach, and the occasional visitor wandered round at a loss, in search of a stamp or a signature for a form.

Finally, Maigret came across a police officer who recognized him.

'Inspector Vanneau?'

'Second corridor on the left, third door down.'

'Could you fetch him for me? He will have someone in his office with him. Don't mention my name out loud.'

Vanneau joined him a few moments later.

'Is he here?'

'Yes.'

'How did it go?'

'Just so-so. I made sure to arm myself with a police summons. I rang his bell. A maid opened the door, and I asked to see her employer. I had to wait a few minutes in the hallway. Then he came downstairs, and I handed him the paper. He read it and looked at me without a word.

'"If you would care to accompany me, I have a car outside."

'He shrugged his shoulders and took a panama hat from the coat stand, put it on his head and followed me.

'He's now sitting in my office. Hasn't unclenched his teeth yet.'

A few moments later, Maigret entered Vanneau's office, where he found Serre smoking a very black cigar. Maigret went and sat in Vanneau's chair.

'I am very sorry for having disturbed you, Monsieur Serre, but I would like you to answer a few questions.'

As on the previous day, the enormous dentist gave him a lugubrious look, and there wasn't a trace of warmth in those dark eyes. Maigret suddenly remembered what he reminded him of: one of those Turks you used to see in pictures. The girth, the obvious weight, the physical force too, no doubt. For, despite his fatness, he gave the impression of being very strong. He also displayed the haughty calm of those pashas that adorn cigarette packets.

Instead of giving a sign of assent, or making some conventional polite remark, or even protesting, Serre took a yellowish piece of paper from his pocket and glanced at it.

'I have been summoned by the chief inspector of Neuilly,' he said. 'I am waiting to hear what said person requires of me.'

'By that do I take it that you refuse to answer any of my questions?'

'Absolutely.'

Maigret hesitated. He had seen all sorts in his time: the tough ones, the stubborn ones, the obstinate ones, the sly ones, but none of them had ever responded to him with such total composure.

'I suppose there's no point in insisting?'

'In my opinion, no.'

'Or to suggest that your lack of cooperation does you no favours?'

This time the man merely sighed.

'Very well. Wait here. The chief inspector will see you.'

Maigret went to find him. The latter didn't understand what was being asked of him at first, then only agreed to it with bad grace. His office was more comfortable and luxurious than the rest of the building; he had a marble clock on his mantelpiece.

'Send Monsieur Serre in,' he told the orderly.

He showed him to a red velvet chair.

'Sit down, please, Monsieur Serre. This is simply to verify a few facts, and I won't take up too much of your time.'

The chief inspector consulted a piece of paper that had just been handed to him.

'Are you the owner of a car with the registration number RS 8822L?'

The dentist nodded. Maigret had gone to sit on the window-sill and watched him, deep in thought.

'Is this car still in your possession?'

Another nod.

'When did you last use it?'

'I presume I have a right to know the purpose of these questions?'

The inspector wriggled on his seat. He wasn't at all pleased with the task that Maigret had handed him.

'Suppose that your car was involved in an accident.'

'Was it?'

'Suppose that a car with this number has been reported as having knocked someone down.'

'When?'

The inspector cast a reproachful look at Maigret.

'Tuesday evening.'

'Where?'

'Near the Seine.'

'My car never left its garage on Tuesday evening.'

'Someone could have used it without your knowledge.'

'I don't think so. The garage is locked.'

'So you confirm that you didn't use your car on Tuesday evening or later that night?'

'Who witnessed the accident?'

The inspector cast another helpless look in the direction of Maigret, who, realizing that this was going nowhere, signalled to him not to persist.

'I have no more questions to ask, Monsieur Serre. Thank you for your time.'

The dentist got up, seeming for a moment to fill the whole office with his bulk, put on his hat and left, giving Maigret a look as he went.

'I did everything I could. As you saw.'

'I saw.'

'Did you derive anything useful from it?'

'Perhaps.'

'He's trouble, that one. He knows his rights.'

'I know.'

It was as if Maigret were inadvertently aping the dentist. He had that same heavy, sombre manner. He headed for the door in turn.

'What's he supposed to have done, Maigret?'

'I don't know yet. It's possible he killed his wife.'

He went to thank Vanneau then headed outside, where his police car awaited. Before getting back in the car, he had a drink at the bar on the corner. He viewed his reflection in the mirror behind the bar and wondered what he would look like in a panama hat. Then he had a smile to himself at the thought that what was about to take place was a fight between heavyweights.

He told the driver:

'Take Rue de la Ferme.'

Not far from number 43a he spotted Serre walking along the pavement in long, slightly loose strides. Like many large men, he spread his legs wide. He was still smoking his long cigar. As he passed the garage he couldn't have failed to notice the police officer on watch there, who had nowhere to hide.

Maigret decided against stopping the car outside the house with the black gate. What would be the point? They probably wouldn't allow him to come in.

Ernestine was waiting in the glass-sided waiting room at Quai des Orfèvres. He showed her into his office.

'Any news?' she asked.

'Not a thing.'

He was in a bad mood. She wasn't to know that he was quite used to being in a bad mood at the beginning of a tricky investigation.

'I received a postcard this morning. I've brought it with me.'

She showed him a postcard in colour of the town hall in Le Havre. There was nothing written on it, no signature, nothing but the poste restante address of La Grande Perche.

'Alfred?'

'It's his writing.'

'So he didn't go to Belgium?'

'Looks that way. He must have been wary of the border.'

'Do you think he might be looking for a ship?'

'I don't think so. He's never set foot on a boat. I want to ask you a question, Monsieur Maigret, but you must give me an honest answer. Supposing he came back to Paris, what would happen to him?'

'You want to know whether he will be arrested?'

'Yes.'

'For the attempted burglary?'

'Yes.'

'We couldn't arrest him, because he was not caught in the act, and besides Guillaume Serre hasn't filed a complaint and even denies that he was broken into at all.'

'So he'll be left in peace?'

'As long as he hasn't lied, and something else didn't happen.'

'Can I make him a promise?'

'Yes.'

'In that case I'll insert a small ad in the paper. He reads the same newspaper every day, for the crosswords.'

She observed him for a moment.

'You don't seem too sure.'

'About what?'

'About the case. About yourself. I can't put my finger on it. Did you see the dentist again?'

'Half an hour ago.'

'What did he say?'

'Nothing.'

She didn't press the point, and when the telephone rang she took her cue to leave.

'What is it?' Maigret growled into the receiver.

'It's me, chief. Can I come round to your office?'

A few seconds later Janvier entered the room, animated, looking very pleased with himself.

'I've got stacks of leads. Want to hear them now? Do you have a moment?'

His enthusiasm was somewhat dampened by Maigret, who had taken off his jacket and was now loosening his tie to free his thick neck.

'I went to that family boarding house you mentioned first of all. It's a bit like some of those hotels on the Left Bank, with palm trees in the lobby and old women sitting in rattan chairs. Hardly any of the guests were under fifty. Mainly foreigners – English, Swiss and American women who visit museums and write never-ending letters.'

'Well?'

Maigret knew the type of place. No need for more information.

'Maria Van Aerts lived there for a year. They remember her – she was quite a popular guest. They said she was a happy soul who was always laughing, and her enormous bosom wobbled every time she chuckled. She used to stuff herself with cakes and went to all the lectures at La Sorbonne.'

'Is that all?' said Maigret, in a voice that made clear that he didn't see what all the excitement was about.

'Every day she wrote eight- to ten-page letters.'

Maigret shrugged his shoulders, then looked at Janvier with new interest. He understood.

'Always to the same person, a friend from the boarding house who now lives in Amsterdam. I have the name. This friend came to see her once. They shared the same room for three weeks. I presume Maria Serre continued to write to her after she was married. The friend's name is Gertrude Oosting. She is the wife of a brewer. It shouldn't be too difficult to find her address.'

'Ring Amsterdam.'

'Would you like the letters?'

'The recent ones, if possible.'

'That's what I thought. Brussels still have no news on Sad Freddie.'

'He's in Le Havre.'

'Should I telephone Le Havre?'

'I'll do it myself. Who's free next door?'

'Torrence returned to the office this morning.'

'Send him in.'

Another heavyweight, who would hardly pass unnoticed on the pavement of an empty street.

'Go and set yourself up in Rue de la Ferme in Neuilly, opposite 43a, a house with a small garden and a black gate at the front. No need to hide. Quite the opposite. If you see a guy who is taller and wider than you, follow him and make sure he sees you.'

'Is that all?'

'Find someone to relieve you for part of the night. There's a Neuilly officer on watch further down the street, opposite the garage.'

'What if the guy drives off?'

'Take a car from downstairs and leave it parked next to the pavement.'

He couldn't face going home for lunch. It was hotter than the day before. There was a storm brewing. Most men were carrying their jackets over their arms, and there were children swimming in the Seine.

He went and had a bite to eat in the Brasserie Dauphine, once he had drunk, by way of a challenge, two Pernods. Then he walked up to Criminal Records in the overheated top storey of the Palais de Justice to speak to Moers.

'Let's say about eleven this evening. Take whatever equipment you need. Take someone with you.'

'Yes, chief.'

He had alerted the police in Le Havre. Did Sad Freddie take a train from Gare du Nord after all – to Lille, say – or did he, for example, head across to Gare Saint-Lazare after his phone call to Ernestine?

He was probably holed up in some cheap rented room or else was wandering from bar to bar drinking bottles of Vichy water, assuming he wasn't trying to stow away on some ship. Was it just as hot in Le Havre as here in Paris?

They still hadn't tracked down the taxi that was supposed to have taken Maria Serre and her luggage. The staff at Gare du Nord didn't remember seeing her. Opening his newspaper around three o'clock, Maigret saw Ernestine's small ad:

For Alfred. Return Paris. No danger. All sorted. Tine.

It was four thirty when he found himself in his chair, the newspaper on his lap. He hadn't turned the page. He had fallen asleep; his mouth was sticky, his back was stiff.

There weren't any police cars available, so he had to take a taxi at the end of the street.

'Rue de la Ferme, Neuilly. I'll tell you where to stop.'

He almost dozed off again. It was five to five when he stopped the taxi in front of the bar that was already so familiar to him. There was no one out on the terrace. He could see the broad silhouette of Torrence walking up and down in the shade further along the street. He paid the driver and sat himself down with a satisfied sigh.

'What can I get you, Monsieur Maigret?'

A beer, of course! He was so thirsty he could drink five or six glasses in one go.

'Has he come back?'

'The dentist? No. I saw his mother, this morning, walking down towards Boulevard Richard-Wallace.'

The gate creaked. A small, nervous-looking woman started walking down the opposite pavement. Maigret paid for his drink and caught up with her when she reached the edge of the Bois de Boulogne.

'Madame Eugénie?'

'What do you want?'

It seemed charm was in short supply at the Serre residence.

'I'd like a little chat with you.'

'I don't have time for a chat. I have to do my own house-work when I get home.'

'I'm from the police.'

'Makes no difference.'

'I need to ask you some questions.'

'Do I have to reply?'

'It would be better if you did.'

'I don't like the police.'

'That's your prerogative. Do you like your employers?'

'They're scum.'

'Old Madame Serre too?'

'She's a bitch.'

They reached the bus stop. Maigret hailed a passing taxi.

'I'll give you a lift home.'

'I don't much care to be seen with a cop, but a lift's not to be sniffed at, I suppose.'

She climbed into the taxi in stately fashion.

'What have you got against them?'

'What about you? Why are you sticking your nose into their business?'

'Has young Madame Serre gone away?'

'Young?' she said sarcastically.

'Let's call her the daughter-in-law.'

'Yes, she's gone. Good riddance.'

'Was she a bitch too?'

'No.'

'You didn't like her?'

'She was always ferreting about in the larder. Come dinner time, I'd find half of what I'd prepared had gone.'

'When did she leave?'

'Tuesday.'

They were crossing Pont de Puteaux. Eugénie tapped on the window.

'It's here,' she said. 'Do you need me any more?'

'Can I come in for a moment?'

They were on a crowded square. The cleaning lady made for a doorway to the right of a shop, went in and headed up a stairway that smelled of dishwater.

'I just wish you could tell them to leave my son in peace.'

'Tell who?'

'The other cops. The local ones. They're always on his back.'

'What's he done?'

'He works.'

'Doing what?'

'How would I know? If the place is a mess, that's too bad. I can't clean all day for them and keep my own place clean as well.'

She opened the window, because it was stuffy in there, but the room was perfectly tidy, apart from a bed in the corner; it was the sort of living-cum-dining room that even had a certain charm.

'What's going on?' she asked as she removed her hat.

'Maria Serre is missing.'

'Of course, she's in Holland.'

'They can't find her in Holland either.'

'Why do they need to find her?'

'Because there is reason to believe that she has been murdered.'

There was a small sparkle in Eugénie's dark-brown eyes.

'Why don't you arrest them?'

'We don't have any proof yet.'

'And you're hoping I can provide you with some?'

She put some water to boil on the gas stove then returned to Maigret.

'What happened on Tuesday?'

'She spent all day packing her bags.'

'Just a moment. She has been married for two years, is that right? I'd imagine that she owned a certain number of personal effects.'

'She had at least thirty dresses and as many pairs of shoes.'

'Was she fond of clothes?'

'She never threw anything away. Some of her dresses were ten years old. She didn't wear them any more, but wouldn't have given them away for all the tea in China.'

'She was a hoarder?'

'Aren't all rich people?'

'I was told she took only a trunk and two suitcases.'

'That's right. The rest was sent a week earlier.'

'You mean she sent other trunks?'

'Trunks, crates, cardboard boxes. A removal lorry came to pick it all up last Thursday or Friday.'

'Did you look at the labels?'

'I don't remember the exact address, but they were bound for Amsterdam.'

'Did your employer know that?'

'Of course.'

'So her departure had been planned for a while?'

'Since her last attack. Every time she had an attack she spoke of going back to her own country.'

'What sort of attack?'

'Heart. That's what she said.'

'She had a bad heart?'

'So it seems.'

'Did a doctor come and see her?'

'Doctor Dubuc.'

'Was she taking medication?'

'With every meal. They all did. The other two still do. They each had their little bottle of pills or drops next to their plates.'

'Is Guillaume Serre ill?'

'I don't know.'

'His mother?'

'Rich people always have something or other.'

'Did they get on?'

'There were weeks when they didn't talk at all.'

'Did Maria Serre do a lot of writing?'

'From dawn till dusk almost.'

'Did you take her letters to the post office?'

'Often. They were always to the same person, a woman with a funny name who lives in Amsterdam.'

'Are the Serres rich?'

'I guess so.'

'And Maria?'

'Sure she is. Otherwise he wouldn't have married her.'

'Were you working for them when they got married?'

'No.'

'Do you know who was cleaning for them at that time?'

'They're always changing cleaners. It's my last week there. As soon as you see how things really are there, you leave.'

'Why?'

'How would you feel if your employer counted every last sugar lump in the bowl and gave you half-rotten apples for dessert?'

'Old Madame Serre?'

'Yes. She makes out she works every hour of the day at her age, which is her choice, and then she's on your back if you as much as sit down for a moment's breather.'

'Does she scold you?'

'She's never scolded me. I'd like to see her try! No, it's worse than that. She's ultra-polite, she gives you a sort of sorry look as if the very sight of you makes her depressed.'

'Did anything strike you in particular when you went to work on Wednesday morning?'

'No.'

'Did you perhaps notice that one of the windowpanes had been broken during the night, or that there was fresh putty round one of the panes?'

She nodded.

'Yes, but you've got the wrong day.'

'Which day was it?'

'Two or three days earlier, after that big storm.'

'Are you sure?'

'Positive. I even had to polish the floor of the study because the rain had got into the house.'

'Who replaced the pane?'

'Monsieur Guillaume.'

'Did he go and buy it himself?'

'Yes. He got some putty as well. It was about ten in the morning. He must have gone to the hardware shop on Rue de Longchamp. If they can avoid paying for a handyman, they will. Monsieur Guillaume unblocks the drains himself.'

'You're sure of the date?'

'Positive.'

'Thank you.'

There was nothing else for Maigret to do here. There was nothing else in Rue de la Ferme either, in fact. Unless Eugénie was merely repeating what she had been told to say, in which case she was a better liar than the rest of them.

'You don't think they might have killed her, do you?'

He didn't reply but headed for the door.

'Because of the windowpane?'

There was a note of hesitancy in her voice.

'Does it matter which day the window was broken on?'

'Why do you ask? Would you like to see them go to prison?'

'Nothing I'd like better. But now I've told you what really happened . . .'

She was regretting having said it. She looked as if she would have changed her story at the drop of a hat.

'You could always check at the hardware shop where he bought the glass and putty.'

'Thank you for the advice.'

He paused for a moment outside the building, which was, as it turned out, a hardware shop, but not the right one. He waited for a taxi.

'Rue de la Ferme.'

It wasn't worth keeping Torrence and the officer from Neuilly kicking their heels on the pavement any longer. He recalled Ernestine's little comedy on Rue de la Lune, but not with amusement. He started thinking about her. She was the one who had set him off on this chase. He had been stupid to lend it so much weight. Just that morning he had made a complete fool of himself in the office of the Neuilly detective chief inspector.

His pipe didn't taste good. He crossed and uncrossed his legs. The window between him and the driver was open.

'Go to Rue de Longchamp. If the hardware shop is still open, pull up there a moment.'

It was his last throw: heads or tails. If the shop was shut, he wouldn't bother coming back, despite all the Ernestines and Sad Freddies. What proof was there that Alfred really had broken into the house in Rue de la Ferme?

True, he had set off from Quai de Jemmapes on his bicycle and in the early hours had telephoned his wife. But no one knew for sure what they had said to each other.

'It's open!'

He meant the hardware shop. A tall youth in a grey overall emerged from the stacks of galvanized pails and brushes to greet him.

'Do you sell window glass?'

'Yes, monsieur.'

'And putty?'

'Of course. Do you have the dimensions?'

'It's not for me. Do you know Monsieur Serre?'

'The dentist? Yes, monsieur.'

'Is he one of your customers?'

'He has an account here.'

'Have you seen him recently?'

'Not me, but I only got back from holiday the day before yesterday. He may have come when I was away. It's easy to check, I just need to consult the book.'

Without asking any questions, the shop assistant went into the semi-darkness of the shop and opened a ledger that was resting on a tall desk.

'He bought a pane of glass last week.'

'Can you tell me which day?'

'Friday.'

The storm had been on Thursday evening. Eugénie had been right, and old Madame Serre!

'He also bought a half-pound of putty.'

'Thank you.'

And then, a hair's breadth away from being missed entirely: the young man, who was no doubt keen to close up the shop, mechanically turned a page, just to be conscientious. He said:

'He came again this week.'

'Huh?'

'Wednesday. He bought a pane of the same dimensions, forty-two by sixty-five, and another half-pound of putty.'

'Are you certain?'

'I can even tell you that he came first thing, because it's the first sale of the day.'

'What time do you open?'

This was important, because Eugénie, who started work at nine o'clock, claimed that she found all the panes intact on Wednesday morning.

'The staff come in at nine, but the owner opens the shop at eight.'

'Thank you very much. You're an excellent fellow.'

The excellent fellow must have scratched his head long and hard about why this man, who had seemed so mournful when he came in, suddenly perked up at this piece of information.

'I take it there is no reason why you would tear out the pages from this ledger?'

'Why would we do that?'

'Indeed! Nevertheless, I would recommend that you take good care of it. I will send someone over tomorrow to take photographs.'

He took a card from his pocket and handed it to the young man, who was amazed to read:

Divisional Detective Chief Inspector Maigret
Police Judiciaire
Paris

'Where now?' asked the driver.

'Stop for a moment in Rue de la Ferme. You will see a small bistro on the left-hand side . . .'

This was worth celebrating with a beer. He nearly called Torrence and the other officer to share one with him, but in the end he settled for the driver.

'What'll you have?'

'A white wine and Vichy.'

The street was golden in the sunlight. They could hear the rustle of the breeze in the tall trees of the Bois de Boulogne.

There was a black gate further down the street, and behind it a square of lawn and a house as calm and as well ordered as a convent.

And in this house there was an old woman who resembled a mother superior and a man who looked like a Turk with whom Maigret had a score to settle. Life was truly good.

5.

The rest of the day went like this. First, Maigret downed two beers in the company of his taxi-driver, who restricted himself to a single white wine and Vichy. It was that time of day when the air starts to feel cooler, and as he got back into the taxi Maigret had the idea of going to the boarding house where Maria Van Aerts had lived for a year.

There was nothing in particular he needed to do there. He would admit it was just his habit of nosing round people's houses to get to know them better.

The walls were a creamy white. Everything was creamy and soft, like an éclair, and the landlady, with her thick-pasted face, looked like an over-iced cake.

'Such a lovely person, Monsieur Maigret! What a marvellous companion she will have made for her husband! She so much wanted to get married.'

'You mean she was looking for a husband?'

'Don't all young girls dream of their Prince Charming?'

'She was forty-eight at the time she lived with you, if I am not mistaken?'

'She was still a young girl inside! The slightest thing would amuse her. She used to play these little tricks on all my lodgers. There's this shop next to the Madeleine that I had never noticed before I met her. They sell all sorts of jokes: fake mice, spoons that melt in your coffee, gadgets you can slide under the tablecloth to lift up someone's plate, glasses you can't drink out of, and all manner of things besides. She was one of that shop's best customers!

'And yet she was a very cultured person; she knew all the museums of Europe and would spend whole days in the Louvre.'

'Did she introduce you to her future husband?'

'No, she was very secretive about that. Perhaps she didn't want to bring him here, where others might have their eye on him. Apparently he was a man with an imposing presence; he came across as a diplomat.'

'Ah.'

'He was a dentist, she told me, but he had just a few select clients, whom he saw by appointment only. He comes from a rich family.'

'And Mademoiselle Van Aerts?'

'Her father left her a tidy sum.'

'Tell me, was she stingy?'

'Has someone been talking to you? It's true she was careful with her money. For example, whenever she had to go into town, she would wait until another resident was going so that she could share the cost of a taxi. And every week she would have something to say about her bill.'

'Do you know how she met Monsieur Serre?'

'I think it was through an ad.'

'She placed lonely hearts ads in the papers?'

'Not in a serious way. She didn't really go in for that sort of thing. It was more as a joke. I don't remember the exact words, but it was something along the lines of "Distinguished, rich foreign lady seeks gentleman of equivalent standing with a view to marriage." She received hundreds of replies. She met her correspondents at the Louvre, in this or that gallery, and they had to be carrying a certain book under their arm or wearing a flower in their buttonhole.'

There were other women like her – from England, Sweden, America – sitting in rattan chairs in the lobby, where there was a background hum of well-oiled electric fans.

'I hope nothing bad has happened to her.'

It was around seven when Maigret stepped out of the taxi on Quai des Orfèvres. In the shade of the pavement he spotted Janvier arriving with a packet under his arm, looking preoccupied, and he waited for him to catch up so that they could mount the stairs together.

'How's it going, Janvier, old man?'

'Fine, chief.'

'What have you got there?'

'My dinner.'

Janvier wasn't one to complain, but today he had a martyred look.

'Why not go home?'

'Because of that damned Gertrude.'

The offices were almost deserted, swept by draughts, because a breeze had picked up, and nearly all the windows of the building had been left open.

'I've managed to track down Gertrude Oosting in Amsterdam. Or rather, I've talked to her maid on the phone. She didn't speak a word of French, so I found this guy who was applying for an identity card at the immigration office and asked him to interpret for me. Then I rang her back.

'As luck would have it, the Oosting woman had gone out with her husband at four p.m. There's some sort of open-air concert on over there today, with a fancy-dress parade, after which the Oostings were due to dine with friends, the maid didn't know where. She didn't know either when they were due to return, and she had been charged with putting the children to bed.

'Talking of children . . .'

'What?'

'Nothing, chief.'

'Spit it out!'

'It's nothing. Just that my wife is disappointed. It's our eldest son's birthday. She has prepared a special dinner. It doesn't matter.'

'Did you ask the maid whether Gertrude Oosting speaks French?'

'She does.'

'Then off with you.'

'What did you say?'

'I said, off you go. Give me your sandwiches, and I'll stay here.'

'Madame Maigret won't be happy.'

Janvier took a bit of persuading, but he eventually set off, dashing to catch his train.

Maigret ate alone in his office, then went to have a chat with Moers in his laboratory. Moers didn't leave until nine o'clock, once night had completely fallen.

'Got that?'

'Yes, chief.'

He took a photographer with him, and masses of equipment. It wasn't strictly legal, but since Guillaume Serre had bought two windowpanes, not one, that scarcely mattered any more.

'Give me Amsterdam, please . . .'

The maid at the other end of the line jabbered away in Dutch, and he thought the gist of it was that Madame Oosting hadn't got home yet.

Then he called his wife.

'Would it put you out to come and have a drink on the terrace of the Brasserie Dauphine? I'll probably be stuck here for another hour or two. Take a taxi.'

It was a reasonably pleasant evening. They were just as comfortable here as in a café on the Grands Boulevards, except that the only view they had was of the tall, pale stairway of the Palais de Justice.

His men would be at work now in Rue de la Ferme. Maigret had instructed them to wait until the Serres had gone to bed. Torrence would keep a lookout in front of the house to make sure they weren't disturbed, and the others would go into the garage, which could be seen from the windows of the house, and give the car a thorough going-over. This was a job for Moers and the photographer. They would take everything: fingerprints, dust samples, the whole works.

'You look happy.'

'Well, I'm not unhappy.'

He didn't tell her that, just a few hours earlier, he was far from being in a good humour. He started drinking shorts, while his wife was content with a herbal tea.

He left her twice to go up to his office to ring Amsterdam. It was eleven thirty before a voice that was not that of the maid replied to him in French.

'I can't hear you very well.'

'I said, I am ringing from Paris.'

'Oh! Paris!'

She had a strong accent, which was not unattractive.

'Police Judiciaire.'

'Police?'

'Yes. I am ringing you about your friend Maria. You know Maria Serre, is that right? Maiden name Van Aerts.'

'Where is she?'

'I don't know. That's what I'm asking you. Did she write to you often?'

'Often, yes. I was meant to meet her from the train on Wednesday morning.'

'Did you wait for her?'

'Yes.'

'Did she come?'

'No.'

'Did she send you a telegram or phone you to say she wouldn't be coming?'

'No. I am worried.'

'Your friend has disappeared.'

'What do you mean?'

'What did she say to you in her letters?'

'Lots of things.'

She started speaking to someone next to her – probably her husband – in her own language.

'Do you think Maria is dead?'

'Perhaps. Did she ever express any discontent when she wrote to you?'

'She wasn't happy.'

'Why?'

'She didn't like the old woman.'

'Her mother-in-law?'

'Yes.'

'And her husband?'

'It turns out he isn't a man, but a child who is very scared of his mother.'

'Has she been writing to you about this for a long time?'

'Since almost straight after her marriage. A few weeks after.'

'Was she already talking about leaving him?'

'Not at that stage. After a year or so.'

'And recently?'

'She made her mind up. She asked me to find her an apartment in Amsterdam, near where we live.'

'Did you find her one?'

'Yes, and a maid.'

'So everything was in place?'

'Yes. I was at the station.'

'Would it bother you to send me copies of the letters you received from your friend? Have you kept them?'

'I keep all the letters, but it would be a huge task to get them all copied; they are very long. I can send you the main ones. Are you sure she has met with some misfortune?'

'I'm convinced of it.'

'Has she been killed?'

'It's very likely.'

'Her husband?'

'I don't know. Listen, Madame Oosting, could you do me a big favour? Does your husband have a car?'

'Of course.'

'Would he be so kind as to drive you to the central police headquarters, which remains open all night? Tell the inspector that you were expecting your friend Maria. Show him her last letter. Say that you are extremely worried and that you would like the matter looked into.'

'Should I mention you?'

'That isn't necessary. The important thing is that you request an investigation.'

'I'm on my way.'

'Thank you. Don't forget the letters you promised to send me.'

He immediately rang Amsterdam again – the police this time.

'In a few minutes you will receive a visit from a certain Madame Oosting, who will tell you about the disappearance of her friend Madame Serre, née Van Aerts.'

'Did she disappear in Holland?'

'No, in Paris. But in order to proceed I need an official complaint. As soon as you log her statement, I would like you to send me a telegram, asking us to initiate an investigation.'

This all took a little time. The inspector at the other end of the line couldn't fathom how Maigret, in Paris, could know Madame Oosting was about to pay a visit.

'I will explain later. All I need from you is a telegram. Mark it top priority. I will get it in less than half an hour.'

He went back to Madame Maigret, who was languishing on the terrace of the brasserie.

'Have you finished?'

'Not yet. I'll have one more drink, then we'll go.'

'Home?'

'To my office.'

That always impressed her. Only rarely had she got inside the inner sanctum of Quai des Orfèvres and she never quite knew how to behave there.

'You seem to be enjoying yourself. As if you were planning a trick on someone.'

'You're not far off the mark.'

'Who is it?'

'A man who is a cross between a Turk, a diplomat and a small child.'

'I don't understand.'

'Of course you don't!'

He was rarely in such good humour. How many glasses of calvados had he drunk? Four? Five? This time, before going back to the office, he downed a beer, then he took his wife's arm and walked her along the two hundred metres of embankment that separated them from the Police Judiciaire.

'I want to ask just one thing: don't start going on again about how dusty it is and how all the offices need a thorough clean.'

On the telephone:

'No telegrams for me?'

'Nothing, inspector.'

Ten minutes later, the whole team, apart from Torrence, got back from Rue de la Ferme.

'How did it go? Any hitches?'

'No hitches. Nobody interrupted us. Torrence insisted that we wait until all the lights went out in the house, and Guillaume Serre took ages to go to bed.'

'The car?'

Vacher, who had nothing more to do, asked permission to go home. That left Moers and the photographer. Madame Maigret, sitting on a chair like a visitor, looked around idly and pretended not to listen.

'We examined the whole car. It seems not to have been used for two or three days. The tank was half full. Nothing disturbed on the inside. I found two or three recent scratches on the boot.'

'As if someone had loaded a heavy piece of luggage?'

'It could have been something like that.'

'A trunk, for example?'

'A trunk or a crate.'

'Any spots of blood on the inside?'

'No. No hairs either. I thought of that. We took a spot-light with us, and there is a plug socket in the garage. Émile will develop the photos.'

'I'll go and do that now,' said the photographer. 'If you don't mind waiting twenty minutes or so . . .'

'I'll wait. Moers, did you get the impression that the car had been cleaned recently?'

'Not on the outside. It hasn't been washed in a garage. But it seems that the inside has been meticulously swept. They must have taken out the floor mat and beaten it, because I had trouble finding any dust to collect. I did, however, pick up a few samples, which I will analyse.'

'Is there a brush in the garage?'

'No. I looked. They must have taken it away.'

'So, apart from the scratches . . .'

'Nothing out of the ordinary. Can I go upstairs now?'

Then they were alone in the office, he and Madame Maigret.

'Are you tired?'

She said that she wasn't. She had a particular way of looking at the surroundings in which her husband spent the greater part of his life and which were so unfamiliar to her.

'Is it always like this?'

'What?'

'An investigation. When you don't come home.'

She must be finding it very calm, very easy, little more than a game, really.

'It depends.'

'Is it to do with a murder?'

'It's more than likely.'

'Do you know who did it?'

He looked at her with a smile, and she averted her gaze. Then she asked:

'Does he know that you suspect him?'

He nodded his head.

'Do you think that he is asleep?'

A moment later, with a shudder, she added:

'It must be awful.'

'It can't have been much fun for the poor woman either.'

'I know, but at least that was probably quicker, wasn't it?'

'Maybe.'

The telegram from the Dutch police was phoned through – the hard copy would arrive the next morning.

'That's it! We can go home now.'

'I thought you were waiting for some photographs.'

He smiled again. She was curious to know the result. She had no desire for sleep.

'They won't tell us anything.'

'You think not?'

'I'm sure of it. Nor will Moers' tests.'

'Why? Did the killer take precautions?'

He didn't reply. He turned out the light and escorted his wife into the corridor, where the cleaners were starting to get to work.

'Is that you, Monsieur Maigret?'

He looked at the alarm-clock, which showed 8.30. His wife had let him sleep in. He recognized Ernestine's voice.

'I haven't woken you, have I?'

He decided to say no.

'I'm at the post office. There's another card for me.'

'From Le Havre?'

'From Rouen. It doesn't say anything, and there's no mention of my ad. Nothing but my poste restante address, like yesterday.'

There was a silence. Then she asked:

'Do you have any news?'

'Yes.'

'What, then?'

'It's all about windowpanes.'

'Good news?'

'Depends for whom.'

'For us?'

'I believe it's good news for you and Alfred, yes.'

'You no longer believe that I was lying to you?'

'Not at present.'

At the office he picked out Janvier to come along with him. The latter took the wheel of the small black police car.

'Rue de la Ferme.'

With the telegram in his pocket, he had Janvier pull up outside the black gate. The pair of them adopted their most professional air and marched in. Maigret rang the bell. A curtain twitched on the first floor, where the shutters were still open. Eugénie answered the door wearing a pair of slippers and wiping her hands on her apron.

'Good morning, Eugénie. Monsieur Serre is at home and I would like to speak to him.'

Someone leaned over the banister. An old woman's voice said:

'Show the gentlemen into the living room, Eugénie.'

It was the first time Janvier had been inside the house, and he was impressed. They listened to the comings and goings above their heads. Then, all of a sudden, the door opened, and the enormous bulk of Guillaume Serre filled almost the entire doorway.

He was just as calm as the day before and was giving them the same insolent stare.

'Do you have a warrant?' he asked, his lip trembling slightly.

With deliberate slowness, Maigret took his wallet from his pocket, opened it, found the piece of paper and handed it over politely.

'Here you are, Monsieur Serre.'

The man wasn't expecting this. He read the slip of paper, then took it over to the window to decipher the signature. Maigret said:

'As you see, it is a search warrant. A case has been opened on the disappearance of Madame Maria Serre, née Van Aerts, following a statement from Madame Gertrude Oosting of Amsterdam.'

The old woman entered as he said these words.

'What is it, Guillaume?'

'Nothing,' he said in a surprisingly gentle voice. 'I believe these gentlemen wish to visit the house. Please go to your room.'

She hesitated and looked at Maigret, as if for advice.

'You will stay calm, won't you, Guillaume?'

'Yes, Mother. Now leave us, please.'

This wasn't going the way Maigret had imagined, and he frowned.

'I suppose,' he said once the old woman had reluctantly torn herself away, 'that you would like to contact a lawyer. I will shortly have a number of questions to ask you.'

'I don't need a lawyer. Since you have a warrant, I can't object to you being here. That's all there is to it.'

The downstairs shutters were closed. The room had been in semi-darkness until that point. Serre went over to the first window.

'No doubt you'd like some light to see by?'

His voice was flat and neutral. If there was any hint of emotion to be perceived there, it was a vague disdain.

'Do your work, gentlemen.'

It was something of a shock to see the living room in broad daylight. Serre went into the study next door, where he also opened the shutters, then into his surgery.

'Let me know when you want to look upstairs.'

Janvier cast a surprised glance at his chief. Maigret no longer seemed to be in his good mood of the morning, or the previous evening. He seemed to have something on his mind.

'Would you allow me to use your phone, Monsieur Serre?' he asked with the same cold politeness that the other man had shown him.

'It's your right.'

He rang the number of the Police Judiciaire. That morning, Moers had made a verbal report, which, as Maigret had expected, was more or less negative. A close examination of the dust had revealed nothing. Or rather, almost nothing. Moers had managed to collect an infinitesimal quantity of powdered brick from under the driver's seat.

'Put me through to the lab. Is that you, Moers? Could you come to Rue de la Ferme with your men and your equipment?'

He kept his eye on Serre, who was lighting a long black cigar and not showing the slightest reaction.

'Bring the lot! No, there is no body. I'll be here.'

Then, turning to Janvier:

'You can begin.'

'In this room?'

'Wherever you like.'

Guillaume Serre followed them round and watched what they were doing without saying a word. He wasn't wearing a tie and he had slipped a black alpaca jacket on over his white shirt.

While Janvier was searching the drawers in the study, Maigret flicked through the dentist's patient records and made some notes in his large notebook.

In truth, it was little more than play-acting. He would be hard put to say what exactly he was looking for. Basically it was a test to see whether at any given moment, in any particular part of the house, Serre would display any signs of nervousness. When they searched the living room, for example, he hadn't turned a hair but had merely stood there, motionless and impassive, with his back to the brown marble mantelpiece.

Now he was staring at Maigret as if wondering what he might be searching for among his papers, but he seemed more curious than afraid.

'You don't have many patients, Monsieur Serre.'

He shrugged his shoulders but didn't reply.

'I note that you have significantly more female patients than male.'

Serre merely glared at him as if to say: 'So what?'

'I note also that you first met Maria Van Aerts in your capacity as a dentist.'

She had made five visits in all, over a space of two months; the records showed the treatment she had received.

'Did you know that she was rich?'

Another shrug.

'Do you know Doctor Dubuc?'

He nodded.

'He is your wife's doctor, if I am not mistaken. Was it you who introduced him to her?'

Finally, he said something!

'Doctor Dubuc tended to Maria Van Aerts before she became my wife.'

'When you married her, were you aware that she had a heart condition?'

'She had spoken to me about it.'

'Was her condition serious?'

'Dubuc will fill you in if he sees fit.'

'Your first wife had heart problems too, didn't she?'

'You will find her death certificate among my papers.'

Janvier was the one who felt most ill at ease. He was happy when the specialists from Criminal Records arrived and relieved the heavy atmosphere somewhat. When the car pulled up outside the gate, Maigret went to open the door himself and said to Moers in a low voice:

'The full works. Go over the house with a fine tooth-comb.'

Moers got the message. Seeing the heavy silhouette of Guillaume Serre, he murmured:

'Do you think that will impress him?'

'I think it'll impress somebody, in the end.'

A few minutes later it was as if auctioneers had moved into the house with a view to putting all the contents up for sale. The forensics team left no stone unturned. They took down the portraits and the pictures, moved the piano and the furniture to look under the carpets, emptied out drawers, spread out papers.

At one point they caught sight of Madame Serre, who popped her head round the door to see what was going on, then went away again, looking upset. Then Eugénie turned up and grumbled:

'I hope you're going to put all that away again when you're finished.'

She complained some more when her kitchen was searched, even down to the broom cupboard.

'If you just told me what you are looking for.'

They weren't looking for anything in particular. Perhaps, if he was honest, Maigret wasn't looking for anything at all. He was observing the man who was following in their tracks and who never let his calm demeanour slip for a moment.

Why had Maria written to her friend that Serre was nothing but an overgrown child?

While the men were working, Maigret picked up the telephone and got Doctor Dubuc on the other end of the line.

'Will you be at home for a while? Can I come and see you? No, it won't take long. I'll tell the maid, thanks.'

Dubuc had five patients in his waiting room and he told the inspector that he would let him in through the back door. It was a short distance away, on the riverside. Maigret went there on foot. On the way he passed by the hardware shop, where the young assistant of the day before waved to him.

'Weren't you going to take photographs of the book?'

'Soon.'

Dubuc was a man in his fifties with a red goatee and glasses.

'You were Madame Serre's physician, is that right, doctor?'

'The young Madame Serre, or at least the younger.'

'Did you ever treat anyone else in the house?'

'Let's see. Yes. There was a cleaning lady who cut her hand, about two or three years ago.'

'Was Maria Serre really ill?'

'She was in need of treatment, yes.'

'Heart?'

'Enlargement of the heart, yes. She also ate too much and complained of dizzy spells.'

'Did she call you often?'

'About once a month. Other times, she came to see me.'

'Did you prescribe any medicine for her?'

'A sedative in pill form. Nothing too strong.'

'Do you believe her heart could have given out?'

'Definitely not. Another ten or fifteen years, maybe . . .'

'Did she never attempt to lose weight?'

'Every four or five months she would say that she was going on a diet, but her resolution never lasted more than a few days.'

'Have you met her husband?'

'I've had occasion.'

'What did you think of him?'

'From what point of view? Professionally? One of my patients was treated by him and said he was very skilful and gentle.'

'And as a man?'

'He strikes me as a very unsociable type. What has happened to him?'

'His wife has disappeared.'

'Ah!'

Dubuc couldn't give a damn, in all honesty, and made only a token gesture of concern.

'These things happen. He was wrong to call the police in. She won't forgive him.'

Maigret decided not to insist. On his way back to the house, he made a detour past the garage; there was no one posted there any more. The building opposite was an apartment block. The concierge was on the doorstep, polishing the brass knob on her door.

'Does your lodge look out on to the street?' he asked.

'What's that to you?'

'I'm with the police. Could you tell me if you know the person who parks his car in the garage opposite, the first on the right?'

'That's the dentist.'

'Do you see him from time to time?'

'I see him when he comes to collect his car.'

'Have you seen him this week?'

'Hey, tell me, what was going on in his garage last night? Was it burglars? I said to my husband—'

'It wasn't burglars.'

'Was it you?'

'It doesn't matter. Have you seen him use his car this week?'

'I think so.'

'Can you remember what day? What time?'

'It was in the evening, quite late. Hold on. I'd just got up. Don't look at me like that. It'll come back to me.'

She seemed to be doing some mental calculation.

'I got up, in fact, because my husband had a toothache, and I gave him an aspirin. If he was here, he'd be able to tell you straight away which day it was. I even noticed Monsieur Serre's car coming out of his garage and said what a coincidence it was.'

'Because your husband had a toothache?'

'Yes. And at the same time there was a dentist outside the house. It was after midnight. Mademoiselle Germaine came home. So it must have been Tuesday, since she only goes out on a Tuesday evening, to play cards with some friends.'

'Was the car leaving the garage? Not going in?'

'Leaving.'

'Which direction did it drive off in?'

'Towards the Seine.'

'Did you hear the car stop further down the street, for example outside the Serre house?'

'I didn't pay any more attention. I was barefoot, and the floor was cold – we sleep with the window open. What's he done?'

What could Maigret say in response to that? He thanked her and walked off. He crossed the small garden and rang the bell. Eugénie answered the door and gave him a dark, reproachful look.

'The gentlemen are upstairs!' she said in a clipped tone.

So they had checked the ground floor. From the first floor came the sound of heavy footsteps and furniture being shunted around on the floorboards.

Maigret went up and found old Madame Serre sat on a chair in the middle of the landing.

'I don't know where to put myself,' she said. 'It's like having the removal men in. What are they looking for, Monsieur Maigret?'

Guillaume Serre was standing in a sun-filled room, lighting a fresh cigar.

'Why in God's name did we let her go?' the old woman sighed. 'If I'd known, I would have . . .'

But she didn't specify what she would have done if she had known the troubles that the disappearance of her daughter-in-law was to bring on their heads.

6.

In which Maigret makes a decision that amazes his colleagues and where his office takes on the aspect of a boxing ring

It was 3.40 when Maigret decided; 4.25 when the interrogation began. But the solemn moment, almost a moment of high drama, was when he made the decision.

Maigret's attitude came as a surprise to those who were working alongside him in Rue de la Ferme. Ever since the morning there had been something unusual in the way that the inspector had been directing operations. It wasn't the first search of this type in which he had participated, but as it went on it began to take on a character all of its own. It was hard to define. Janvier, perhaps because he knew the chief so well, noticed it first.

When he had set them to work, Maigret had had a merry, almost fierce glint in his eye. He had let them loose on the house like a pack of hounds on the trail of a scent, encouraging them not verbally, but by his whole attitude.

Had it become a personal matter between him and Guillaume Serre? More precisely, would events have played out in the same manner, would Maigret have come to the same decision, at that same moment, if the man from Rue de la Ferme hadn't been a heavyweight like him, both physically and psychologically?

From the start he seemed intent to test himself against him.

At other points, different motives might have been attributed to him: was he perhaps taking some perverse pleasure in turning the house upside down?

They rarely got to work in a home like this, where everything was peaceful and harmonious – a muted harmony in a minor key – where the most old-fashioned objects didn't look ridiculous and out of place, and where, after hours of careful searching, not a single piece of incriminating evidence had been unearthed.

When he spoke, at 3.40, they still hadn't found anything. The investigators were starting to feel a bit awkward and were waiting for the inspector to make his excuses and leave.

What was it that made Maigret's mind up? Did he even know himself? Janvier went as far as to think that he had had one drink too many when, around one o'clock, he had gone to get a bite to eat at the terrace of the bistro across the road. Indeed, when he got back, there was a distinct smell of Pernod on his breath.

Eugénie had not laid the table for her employers. Several times she had come to whisper in the ear of either the old woman or the dentist. Later they saw the old woman eating in the kitchen standing up, as you do when in the mess of moving house, and later still, as Guillaume refused to come downstairs, the cleaning lady had taken him up a sandwich and a cup of coffee.

They were searching the attic now, the most private part of the house, more private even than the bedrooms and the linen closets.

It was huge, illuminated by a pair of dormer windows, which cast two wide rectangles of light on the greyish floor. Janvier had opened two leather rifle cases, and the forensics men had examined the guns.

'Do they belong to you?'

'They belonged to my father-in-law. I have never been hunting.'

An hour later, in Guillaume's room, they had found a revolver, which they examined, and which Maigret had added to the pile of objects to take away for further testing.

There were all sorts in this pile, including the dentist's professional records and, from a writing desk in the old lady's bedroom, the death certificates of her husband and her first daughter-in-law.

They also found a suit with a small tear in the sleeve, which Guillaume Serre claimed not to have worn for more than ten days. They ferreted among the trunks, the chests, the rickety old bits of furniture that had been put up in the attic because they were no longer of use. In the corner there was an old-fashioned child's high chair, with coloured balls in either side of the tray, and a rocking horse which had lost its tail and mane.

The work hadn't stopped at lunchtime. The men had taken it in turns to go to get something to eat, and Moers had made do with a sandwich that the photographer brought back for him.

Around two o'clock the office called Maigret to tell him that a thick envelope had been delivered by air mail from Holland. He had them open it. It was Maria's letters, written in Dutch.

'Find a translator and set him to work.'

'Here?'

'Yes. Don't let him leave until I get back.'

Guillaume Serre's attitude hadn't changed. He followed them, observed their every move, but never seemed the slightest bit perturbed.

He had a particular way of looking at Maigret, and it was clear that, for him, the others didn't matter. This was between the two of them. The other officers were just bit-part players. Even the Police Judiciaire didn't exist. The struggle was more personal than that. There was something in the dentist's eyes that was difficult to pin down: something reproachful or contemptuous.

In any case, he wasn't at all impressed by this show of force. He made no protest, submitting to the invasion of his home and his privacy with a lofty resignation, but without displaying the slightest trace of anxiety.

Was he a weakling or a tough nut? Both hypotheses were equally plausible. He had the physique of a wrestler and the air of a man who was completely sure of himself, yet Maria's description of him as an overgrown child did not seem incongruous. His flesh was pale and unhealthy-looking. In a drawer they had found a pile of doctor's prescriptions, stapled together in several batches, some of them dating back twenty years. You could reconstitute the whole family medical history from those prescriptions, some of which had turned yellow. There was also, in the bathroom on the first floor, a small white-painted cabinet that contained medicine bottles and boxes of pills both recent and old. In this house they never threw anything away, not even old brooms: there was a stack of them in the corner of the attic next to a pile of worn-out shoes on which the leather had grown hard and which would never be of use again.

Each time they moved from one room to start on another, Janvier gave Maigret a look as if to say: 'Still nothing!'

Janvier, it seemed, was still expecting to discover something. Was Maigret, on the other hand, expecting to find nothing? He never appeared surprised, he just watched them work, taking lazy puffs on his pipe, sometimes forgetting to pay the dentist any attention for a quarter of an hour at a time.

They found out about his decision indirectly, which made it all the more striking.

Everyone came down from the attic, where Guillaume Serre had closed the two dormer windows. The mother had come out of her room to see them off. They were standing on the landing among all the mess.

Maigret had turned to Serre and said to him, as if it were the most natural thing in the world:

'Would you care to put on a tie and some shoes?'

Since the morning the man had been wearing slippers.

Serre had got the message, had looked at him, surprised no doubt, not that he let that show in his face. His mother had opened her mouth to speak, to protest or to demand an explanation, and Guillaume had grabbed her by the arm and led her into her room.

Janvier had whispered:

'Are you arresting him?'

Maigret hadn't answered. He didn't know. In truth, he had only just made the decision at that precise moment, standing there on the landing.

'Come in, Monsieur Serre. Please take a seat.'

The clock on the mantelpiece showed 4.25. It was a Saturday. This had only occurred to Maigret when he saw how busy the streets were as they drove across town.

Maigret closed the door. The windows were open, and the papers on the desk fluttered beneath the various objects used to pin them down.

'I asked you to take a seat.'

He then went into the closet to hang up his hat and jacket and to rinse his hands in the enamel basin.

He didn't say a word to the dentist for ten minutes but occupied himself with signing the papers that had been awaiting his attention in his office. He rang for Joseph, gave him the dossier, then, with slow, meticulous movements, filled the half-dozen pipes arranged in a row in front of him.

It was highly unusual for a man in Serre's position to sit there so long without asking what was going on, without losing his nerve, without crossing and uncrossing his legs.

Eventually there was a knock at the door. It was the photographer who had worked with them all day, to whom Maigret had entrusted a mission. He handed Maigret a still damp print of a document.

'Thank you, Dambois. Hang around upstairs, will you? Don't leave without letting me know.'

He waited for the door to close again, lit one of his pipes.

'Would you care to pull up your chair, Monsieur Serre?'

113

They found themselves face to face across the width of the desk. Maigret showed him the print he held in his hand.

He didn't make any comment. The dentist took the photograph, removed his glasses from his pocket, examined it closely, then put it down on the desk.

'I'm listening.'

'I have nothing to say.'

The photograph was of a page from the hardware shop's ledger which recorded the purchase of the second pane of glass and the second half-pound of putty.

'Do you see what this means?'

'Am I to understand that I am being charged?'

Maigret thought for a moment.

'No,' he decided. 'Officially you have been called in as a witness. If you prefer, however, I can charge you, or more precisely ask the public prosecutor to charge you, which would allow you to have a lawyer present.'

'I've already told you that I don't need a lawyer.'

These were nothing more than the opening parries. Two heavyweights sizing each other up, taking each other's measure, probing. The office was like a boxing ring, and outside, in the inspectors' room, where Janvier had just filled in his colleagues, there was total silence.

'I think this is going to be a long one!' he had told them.

'The chief is in it for the long haul.'

'He looks like he means business.'

They all knew what that meant, and Janvier was the first to telephone his wife to tell her not to be surprised if he got home late that night.

'Do you have a heart problem, Monsieur Serre?'

'Enlargement of the heart – like you, no doubt.'

'Your father died of heart disease when you were seventeen, isn't that right?'

'Seventeen and a half.'

'Your first wife died of heart disease. Your second wife also had heart problems.'

'According to official figures, around thirty per cent of people die of heart failure.'

'Do you have life insurance, Monsieur Serre?'

'Since I was a child.'

'Yes, I saw your policy earlier. Your mother, if I recall, is not insured?'

'That is correct.'

'But your father was.'

'I believe so.'

'And your first wife?'

'I saw you take away the relevant documents.'

'What about your second wife?'

'There's nothing unusual in that.'

'What is unusual is to keep a sum amounting to several million, in currency and gold, locked in a safe.'

'Really?'

'Can you tell me why you keep this large sum at home, where it isn't accruing any interest?'

'I would say that thousands of people these days are doing the same. You seem to be forgetting we've undergone financial crises, which have led to crashes, excessive taxes and constant devaluations . . .'

'I see. So you admit that your intention was to conceal your capital to defraud the tax authorities?'

Serre didn't speak.

'Your wife – I mean your second wife, Maria – did she know that you had this money locked away in your safe?'

'Yes, she did.'

'You told her?'

'She had her own money in there until a few days ago.'

He talked slowly, weighing his words before launching them one by one, keeping a serious eye on the inspector.

'I didn't find a pre-marital contract among your papers. Should I conclude from that that you were married under the laws of common property?'

'That is correct.'

'Surprising, given your ages?'

'It was for the reason I have already mentioned. A contract would have forced us to draw up an inventory of our respective assets.'

'Therefore there was no actual joint ownership?'

'We each preserved control of our own affairs.'

Nothing unusual in that, was there?

'Was your wife rich?'

'She was.'

'About the same as you, or richer?'

'About the same.'

'Was her fortune based entirely in France?'

'Only some of it. She had inherited a part share in a cheese-making business from her father.'

'And in what form were the rest of her holdings?'

'Mainly in gold.'

'Even before she met you?'

'I can see where you're going with this. Nevertheless, I will tell you the truth. I was the one who advised her to sell her shares and buy gold.'

'And this gold was kept alongside yours in your safe?'

'Yes.'

'Until when?'

'Tuesday. Early in the afternoon, when she had more or less finished packing, she came downstairs, and I gave her what was hers.'

'So this sum was, by the time of departure, stashed in one of the two suitcases or the trunk?'

'I suppose it must have been.'

'Did she go out before dinner?'

'I didn't hear her go out.'

'So, as far as you know, she didn't go out?'

He nodded.

'Did she make a telephone call?'

'The only telephone in the house is in the study, and she didn't use it.'

'How can I be sure, Monsieur Serre, that the money I found in the safe is your money alone, and not money belonging to both you and your wife?'

Showing no emotion, with the same air of either lassitude or contempt, the dentist took a green notebook from his pocket, which he handed to the inspector. The pages were covered in tiny figures. The column on the left was headed by the letter U, that on the right by the letter M.

'What does "U" signify?'

'"Us". It means Mother and me. We have always shared everything, not distinguishing between what belongs to me and what belongs to her.'

'And the "M" no doubt stands for Maria?'

'Yes, that's right.'

'I see a certain figure that crops up at regular intervals.'

'That's her contribution to the housekeeping.'

'She paid you every month for bed and board?'

'If you wish to put it that way. In reality, she didn't hand over any cash, as her money was already in the safe, I merely debited her account.'

Maigret sat for a few minutes turning the pages of the notebook without saying a word. Then he got up and went into the office next door, where the inspectors, like schoolchildren, all tried to look busy.

In a low voice he gave some instructions to Janvier, thought for a moment about having some beers sent up, then almost mechanically drained the dregs in the glass that was standing on Vacher's desk.

When he returned, Serre, who had not changed position, had lit up one of his long cigars. Not without a certain insolence, he murmured:

'If I may?'

Maigret thought about saying no, but merely shrugged his shoulders.

'Do you have anything to say about that second windowpane, Monsieur Serre?'

'I haven't really thought about it.'

'Then you should. It would be much better for you if you came up with a plausible explanation.'

'I'm not looking for one.'

'Do you still maintain that you replaced the windowpane in your office only once?'

'The morning after the storm.'

'Would you like me to get the Meteorological Office to verify that there was no storm in Neuilly on the night of Tuesday to Wednesday?'

'No point. Unless that would give you pleasure. I am speaking of the storm last week.'

'You went to the hardware shop on Rue de Longchamp and bought a new pane and some putty.'

'As I have already told you.'

'Are you claiming that you have not returned to the shop since then?'

And he slid the photograph of the ledger under his nose.

'Why, in your opinion, would someone go to the bother of buying a second pane of glass and round of putty?'

'I don't know.'

'For what reason did the shopkeeper declare that you came to his shop again around eight o'clock on Wednesday morning?'

'You'd better ask him.'

'When was the last time you used your car?'

'Last Sunday.'

'Where did you go?'

'Mother and I went for a drive for a couple of hours, as we often do on a Sunday.'

'Where did you go?'

'The forest of Fontainebleau.'

'Did your wife come with you?'

'No. She wasn't feeling well.'

'Had you already decided to separate?'

'It was never about a separation. She was tired, depressed. She wasn't getting on with Mother. By mutual agreement we decided that she should return to her own country for a few weeks or months.'

'Yet she took all her money with her?'

'Yes.'

'Why?'

'Because there was a possibility that she wouldn't be coming back. We aren't children. We are capable of seeing things as they are. It was a sort of experiment we were trying out.'

'Tell me, Monsieur Serre, to get to Amsterdam you have to cross two borders, don't you? French customs are very strict about capital being moved out of the country. Didn't your wife fear that her gold might be discovered and confiscated?'

'Do I have to answer that?'

'I think it would be in your interest to do so.'

'Even if I risk legal consequences?'

'They will probably be less serious than being accused of murder.'

'Very well. One of my wife's suitcases had a false bottom.'

'Expressly for this trip?'

'No.'

'She has used it on other occasions?'

'Several.'

'To go over the border?'

'The Belgian border, and one occasion the Swiss border. I'm sure you're aware that, until recently, it was much easier and less troublesome to acquire gold in Belgium and especially Switzerland.'

'Are you admitting your complicity in these capital transfers?'

'I am.'

Maigret got up and went out into the inspectors' room.

'Could you come in a moment, Janvier?'

Then, to Serre:

'My colleague will record this part of our conversation. Please repeat to him exactly what you have just said to me. Then get him to sign his statement, Janvier.'

He went out and got Vacher to show him the office where the translator was working.

He was a small man in glasses who was typing up his translation directly on the machine, stopping every now and again to consult the dictionary that he had brought with him.

There were at least forty letters, most of them are several pages long.

'Where did you begin?'

'At the beginning. I'm on the third letter now. All three date from a little over two and a half years ago. In the first one, the lady tells her friend that she is going to get married, that her future husband is a distinguished man with a fine bearing, from a very good background, and his mother is like some painting or other in the Louvre. I can give you the name of the painter.'

He looked through his papers.

'Clouet. She's always talking about paintings in these letters. Even if she's talking about the weather she'll refer to Monet or Renoir.'

'I'd like you now to start at the end and work backwards.'

'If you like. You realize that, even if I stay here all night, I won't get through all this by tomorrow morning?'

'That's why I'm asking you to begin at the end. What is the date of the last letter?'

'Last Sunday.'

'Could you read it to me quickly?'

'I can give you a rough idea. Wait.

'"Dear Gertrude, Paris has never looked as resplendent as it does this morning. I almost went out with G and his mother to the forest of Fontainebleau, which I imagine has all the splendours of a Corot or a Courbet—"'

'Is there a lot on these splendours?'

'Shall I skip?'

'Please.'

The translator scanned the pages, moving his lips silently, as if he were at mass.

'Here we go:

'"I wonder what effect it will have on me, seeing Holland again and all its pastel shades, but now that the moment approaches, I feel trepidation. After everything that I have written about my life here, about G and about my mother-in-law, you must be wondering what is going on with me and why I'm not feeling happier.

'"Perhaps it's because of my dream last night, which spoiled my day. Do you remember that painting in the museum in The Hague that made us both blush? It had no signature. It was attributed to a painter from the Florentine school whose name I've forgotten and it represents a faun carrying over his shoulder a completely naked woman, who is putting up a struggle. Do you remember it? In my dream the faun had G's face, and he had such a fierce expression that I woke up trembling and bathed in sweat. Not from fear. It was stranger than that. My memory is confused. There was some fear, for sure, but there was another feeling as well. I will try to tell you about it on Wednesday, when we can finally chat properly like we did when you came to see me.

"'I will leave on Tuesday evening. I've made my mind up. There's no going back. So that's only two more days to wait. I have a lot of things to do in that time. The time will fly by. Yet it still seems far off to me, almost unreal.

"'Sometimes I get the feeling, especially since that dream, that something will happen to prevent me leaving.

"'Don't be afraid. My decision is final. I will follow your advice. I can't put up with this life any longer. But—'"

'Are you there, chief?'

It was Janvier, with the statement in his hand.

'I've finished. He's waiting for you.'

Maigret took the sheets of paper, left the translator to his work and went back through the inspectors' room, deep in thought.

No one at this point could guess how long the interrogation was going to take.

Guillaume Serre looked up at Maigret as he came in and picked up a pen from the desk.

'I suppose I have to sign it?'

'Yes. Here. Have you read it?'

'I've read it. Could I ask you for a glass of water?'

'Would you rather have a glass of red wine?'

The dentist looked at him, gave an indecipherable smile, heavy with irony and bitterness.

'Ah, that,' he said disdainfully.

'Yes, that, Monsieur Serre. You are so frightened of your mother that you are reduced to drinking in secret.'

'Was that a question? Do I have to reply?'

'As you wish.'

'You should know that my mother's father was a drunk, as were her two brothers, who are both dead now, and her sister ended her days in a mental asylum. My mother has lived in fear of me being a drinker too, because she is convinced that this is a hereditary trait. When I was a student, she would sit up anxiously waiting for me to return home. She would sometimes wander round the cafés of Boulevard Saint-Michel, where I would be out with friends. There have never been any spirits in the house, and though we have wine in the cellar, she has always carried the key about with her.'

'She allows you a glass of wine with water at each meal, is that correct?'

'I know that she came to see you and talked to you.'

'Did she repeat what she told me?'

'Yes.'

'Do you love your mother a lot, Monsieur Serre?'

'It has mostly been just the two of us, her and me.'

'A bit like a married couple?'

He reddened slightly.

'I don't know what you mean.'

'Is your mother jealous?'

'Excuse me?'

'I asked you whether your mother, as is often the case with a widow and an only son, displays jealous feelings about your relationships. Do you have many friends?'

'Does this bear any relation to the alleged disappearance of my wife?'

'In your house I didn't find a single letter from a friend or a single photograph of you with a bunch of companions of the sort that you find in most people's homes.'

He didn't say anything.

'Nor is there a single photograph of your first wife.'

More silence.

'Another detail struck me, Monsieur Serre. The portrait hanging above the mantelpiece – is that your maternal grandfather?'

'Yes.'

'The one who drank?'

A nod.

'In a drawer I found a number of portraits of you as a child and a young man, portraits of women and men who must be your grandmother, your aunt and your uncles. All on your mother's side. Does it not strike you as odd that there isn't a single portrait of your father and his family?'

'It's never struck me.'

'Were they destroyed after your father died?'

'My mother is better placed than I to answer that question.'

'So you don't remember them being destroyed?'

'I was quite young.'

'You were seventeen. What image of your father did you keep in your head, Monsieur Serre?'

'Is this part of the interrogation?'

'As you see, neither my questions nor your answers are being recorded. Your father was a lawyer?'

'Yes.'

'Did he run his practice himself?'

'Not really. His head clerk took on most of the work.'

'Did he have a social life? Or did he stay at home with the family all the time?'

'He went out a lot.'

'Did he have mistresses?'

'I don't know.'

'Did he die in his bed?'

'On the stairs, going up to bed.'

'Were you at home?'

'I had gone out. When I got back, he had been dead for two hours.'

'Who took care of him?'

'Doctor Dutilleux.'

'Is he still alive?'

'He died at least ten years ago.'

'Were you there when your first wife died?'

He drew his thick eyebrows together and stared hard at Maigret, jutting out his lower lip in an expression of disgust.

'Answer the question, please.'

'I was at home.'

'In which part of the house?'

'In my study.'

'What time was it?'

'Around nine in the evening.'

'Was your wife in her room?'

'She had gone to bed early. She wasn't feeling very well.'

'Had she been feeling unwell for a few days?'

'I don't recall.'

'Was your mother with her?'

'She was upstairs too.'

'With her?'

'I don't know.'

'Was it your mother who called you?'

'I think so.'

'When you got to the room, was your wife already dead?'

'No.'

'Did she die shortly afterwards?'

'Fifteen, maybe twenty minutes later. The doctor rang at the door.'

'Which doctor?'

'Dutilleux.'

'Is he your family doctor?'

'He was even when I was a child.'

'Was he a friend of your father?'

'Of my mother.'

'Does he have children?'

'Two or three.'

'Have you lost touch with them?'

'I didn't know them personally.'

'Why didn't you inform the police that someone had tried to break into your safe?'

'I had nothing to inform them about.'

'What did you do with the tools?'

'Which tools?'

'The ones the burglar left behind when he ran away.'

'I didn't see any tools or any burglar.'

'Did you use your car on the night of Tuesday to Wednesday?'

'No, I didn't.'

'Do you know if anyone else used it?'

'I haven't had a reason to go to the garage since then.'

'When you parked your car last Sunday, were there any scratches on the boot or the right mudguard?'

'I didn't notice anything.'

'Did you or your mother get out of the car at any point?'

He didn't reply.

'I asked you a question.'

'I'm trying to remember.'

'That doesn't seem too difficult to me. You were driving down the Fontainebleau road. Did you set foot on the ground?'

'Yes. We went for a walk in the country.'

'You mean on a country path?'

'A small path between the fields to the right of the road.'

'Would you be able to find this path again?'

'I think so.'

'Was it paved?'

'I don't think so. No. That seems highly unlikely.'

'Where is your wife, Monsieur Serre?'

And the inspector rose to his feet without waiting for a reply.

'Because we have to find her, don't we?'

7.

In which we see first one woman, then another, in the waiting room, one of whom signals to Maigret not to recognize her

At about five o'clock Maigret had got up for a moment to open the door between his office and the inspectors' room and winked at Janvier. A little later, he had got up again to go and close the window, in spite of the heat, because of the noise coming from outside.

At 5.50 he went into the next-door office with his jacket in his hand.

'Over to you!' he said to Janvier.

The latter and his colleagues had understood the situation a long time ago. From the moment back in Rue de la Ferme when the inspector had ordered Serre to follow him, Janvier was sure that he wouldn't be getting away from Quai des Orfèvres any time soon. What did surprise him was that the chief had made the decision so suddenly, without having all the pieces of the jigsaw in his hand.

'She's in the waiting room,' someone whispered in his ear.

'Who?'

'The mother.'

Maigret installed a young officer, Marileux, who knew shorthand, behind the door.

'The same questions?' asked Janvier.

'The same ones. And any others that come into your head.'

The plan was to wear the dentist down. The rest of them would be able to take turns, go and get a coffee or a beer, make contact with the outside world again, while he would be kept for as long as was necessary in the same office, on the same chair.

Maigret went to see the translator first. The latter had decided to take off his jacket and tie.

'What's the story?'

'I've translated the last four letters. There's a bit here in the last but one that might be of interest to you:

'"My mind is made up, Gertrude. I'm still wondering how it came to this. However, I had no dreams last night or, if I did, I don't remember them."'

'Does she talk about dreams a lot?'

'Yes. She often mentions them. She interprets them.'

'Go on.'

'"You have often asked me what's wrong, and I've told you that you were imagining things and that everything was fine. The truth is, I've been trying hard to convince myself that that is true.

'"I swear that, for the last two and a half years, I have done my best to see this as my home and G as my husband.

'"The truth is, you see, that I knew it wasn't true, that I've always been an outsider, even more so than in the boarding house that you know and where you and I had such a happy time together.

'"So how did I suddenly start to see things as they really are?

'"Do you remember when we were little? How we liked to compare everything we saw – people, streets, animals – to the pictures in our albums? We wished real life was like those pictures. Later, when we started visiting museums, it was the paintings that we used as our point of comparison.

'"I did the same here, but I did it deliberately, without really believing it, and this morning I saw my mother-in-law, I saw G, with fresh eyes and with no illusions.

'"I hadn't had any for a long time – illusions, I mean. I want you to understand. I didn't have any illusions, yet I was so reluctant to give them up.

'"It's over. At a stroke I decided to leave. I haven't spoken about it to anyone yet. The old woman doesn't suspect a thing. She is always the same with me: soft and smiling, as long as I do what she wants.

'"*She is the most selfish woman I have ever met.*"

'Those last words are underlined,' said the translator. 'There's more.

'"As for G, I sometimes wonder whether he'd actually be relieved to see me go. He's known since the start that we have nothing in common. I've never been able to get used to the feel of his skin, the smell of him. Can you see now why we don't share the same room, which so surprised you at first?

'"After two and a half years, it is exactly as if I had just met him in the street or in the Métro, and he still makes me shudder every time he comes into my bed, which fortunately is not very often.

'"Between you and me I think the only reason he comes is because he thinks it gives me pleasure, or simply out of a sense of duty.

'"Perhaps his mother tells him to? It's possible. Don't laugh. I don't know what it's like with your husband, but

131

with G he's like a browbeaten child doing his lines. Do you understand what I'm saying?

"'I've often wondered if it was the same with his first wife. I wouldn't be surprised. He'd be like this with anyone. These people – I mean the mother and her son – live in a world of their own and don't need anyone else.

"'It's hard to believe that the old woman was ever married. They never talk about him. Apart from them, there is nobody else in the world except the people in the portraits on the walls, dead people, but people they talk about as if they were more alive than all the living people on earth.

"'I can't take any more, Gertrude. Soon I'll speak to G. I'll tell him that I need to breathe the air of my own country. He'll understand. What I don't know is how he'll summon up the courage to talk to his mother about it—'"

'Is there a lot more?' asked Maigret.

'Seven pages.'

'Carry on translating. I'll be back.'

At the door he turned round.

'If you feel hungry or thirsty, phone down to the Brasserie Dauphine. Order anything you like.'

'Thank you.'

From the corridor he could see through the glass walls of the waiting room old Madame Serre sitting on one of the green velvet chairs. She sat bolt upright, her hands crossed on her lap. When she spotted Maigret she made a move as if to stand up, but he just walked past and headed for the stairs.

The interrogation had barely begun, yet it was still a surprise to see life carrying on as normal outside, in the sunshine, people coming and going, taxis, buses, with men standing on the platform reading their newspapers on the way home from work.

'Rue Gay-Lussac,' he said to the driver. 'I'll tell you where to stop.'

The tall trees in the Jardin du Luxembourg quivered in the breeze, and all the chairs were occupied. There were lots of women in light summer dresses, and a few children were still playing on the paths.

'Is Maître Orin at home?' he asked the concierge.

'He hasn't been out for more than a month, the poor man.'

Maigret suddenly brought him to mind. He was probably the oldest lawyer in Paris. The inspector didn't know his age, but he was already old when he had first come across him, and partially disabled, not that that stopped him smiling and talking about women with a twinkle in his eye.

He lived with a maid who was almost as old as him in a bachelor's apartment stuffed full of books and engravings, which he collected. Most of the prints were rather racy in content.

Orin was sitting in a chair in front of an open window with a blanket over his knees, despite the temperature.

'Well, young man, what ill wind blows you here? I was beginning to think that everybody had forgotten me or else thought I'd croaked years ago and been dispatched to Père-Lachaise. What can I do for you this time?'

He wasn't under any illusion, and Maigret blushed slightly, since it was true he had rarely paid the lawyer a visit without some ulterior motive.

'I was just wondering whether, by any chance, you might have known someone called Serre, who, if I'm not mistaken, died about thirty-two or thirty-three years ago.'

'Alain Serre?'

'He was a lawyer.'

'That was Alain.'

'What sort of man was he?'

'I don't suppose you can tell me what all this is about?'

'His son.'

'Never met the boy. I knew he had a kid, but our paths never crossed. You see, Maigret, Alain and I were part of a fun-loving crowd for whom domestic bliss was not the be-all and end-all. You'd be more likely to find us in our club or backstage at the variety shows. We knew all the dancing girls by their first names.'

He added, with a rather louche smile:

'If you know what I mean!'

'Did you know his wife?'

'I must have been introduced at some point. Didn't she live in Neuilly or somewhere? Alain went out of circulation for a few years. He wasn't the first one to succumb. There were even some who, once they got married, rather looked down their noses at us. I didn't think I'd see him again. Then, a good while afterwards—'

'How long afterwards?'

'I don't know. Let's think. The gang had upped sticks from Faubourg Saint-Honoré to Avenue Hoche by then. Ten, twelve years maybe? Anyway, he came back. He acted a bit oddly at first, as if he was worried we bore him a grudge for jumping ship.'

'Then?'

'Nothing much. He made up for lost time. Let's think. He was with a girl for a while, little singer, big mouth . . . What's her name? . . . We had a nickname for her, something filthy . . . Ah, I can't remember.'

'Did he drink?'

'No more than most. Two or three bottles of champagne occasionally . . .'

'What happened to him?'

'Same thing that happens to us all in the end. He died.'

'Is that all?'

'If you want to know what happened next, young man, you'd better ask him upstairs. This is St Peter's department, not mine. What misdeed is his son supposed to have committed?'

'I don't know yet. His wife has disappeared.'

'A playboy?'

'No. Quite the opposite.'

'Juliette! Bring us something to drink!'

Maigret was stuck there for another quarter of an hour while the old man insisted on searching through his prints for a sketch of the singer.

'I can't promise you that it's a good likeness. But it was done by a very talented fellow one evening when we all had a party at his studio.'

The girl was naked and walking on her hands. Her face was obscured for the simple reason that her hair was trailing along the floor.

'Come again, my dear Maigret. If you'd had the time to share in my humble meal . . .'

A bottle of wine was breathing in a corner of the room, and the apartment was filled with good cooking smells.

The police in Rouen had been no more successful in finding Sad Freddie than that in Le Havre. The ace safe-cracker probably wasn't even still in town. Was he on his way back to Paris? Had he read Ernestine's ad?

Maigret had sent one of his inspectors on a mission along the riverbank.

'Where should I start?'

'As far upstream as you can manage.'

He had telephoned his wife to let her know that he wouldn't be home for dinner.

'Will I see you at all tonight?'

'Maybe not.'

He wasn't too hopeful. He himself knew that he had made a big decision when he tried to move things forwards quickly and hauled in Guillaume Serre for questioning without the slightest shred of evidence.

Now it was too late. He couldn't back down.

He felt weighed down, irritable. He sat down on the terrace of the Brasserie Dauphine but, having read the menu from beginning to end, merely ordered a sandwich and a glass of beer, as he didn't feel at all hungry.

He went back up the stairs at the Police Judiciaire with slow steps. The lamps had been turned on, even though it was still light outside. Once his head emerged at first-floor level he automatically glanced into the waiting room, and the first thing he spotted was that green hat that was really beginning to get on his nerves.

Ernestine was sitting facing Madame Serre, with her hands on her lap, just like the old woman, and with the same patient and resigned look on her face. She spotted him straight away but reacted only with a fixed stare and a slight shake of the head.

He understood this to mean that she didn't want to be recognized. Then she went back to talking to the old woman, as though they had struck up an acquaintance some time earlier.

He shrugged his shoulders and opened the door to the inspectors' room. The stenographer was at work, a wad of paper on his lap. Janvier's weary voice could be heard, along with the beat of his footsteps as he paced up and down in the office.

'You state, Monsieur Serre, that your wife went to hail a taxi at the corner of Boulevard Richard-Wallace. How long was she away from the house?'

Before relieving Janvier, he went upstairs to Moers' attic. The latter was busy filing documents.

'So, my friend, apart from traces of brick dust, you found nothing else in the car?'

'The car had been given a thorough clean.'

'Are you sure?'

'I was lucky to find the brick dust. It was caught in a fold in the mat under the driver's seat.'

'What if the car hadn't been cleaned and the driver had got out on a country road?'

'A paved road?'

'No. As I say, let us assume that he and the person who was with him got out to go for a walk on this path and then got back into the car.'

'And the car didn't get cleaned afterwards?'

'Yes.'

'There would be traces. Maybe not a lot. But I would have found them.'

'That's all I needed to know. Don't leave yet.'

'Understood. By the way, I found two hairs in the room of the woman who disappeared. She was a natural blonde, but dyed her hair a strawberry blonde. I also know the make of rice powder that she used.'

Maigret walked back downstairs and this time went into his office, removing his jacket as he entered. He had been smoking his pipe all afternoon. Janvier had been smoking cigarettes, and Serre, cigars. The air was blue with smoke, which hung around the light like a fog.

'Are you thirsty, Monsieur Serre?'

'Your inspector gave me a glass of water.'

Janvier went out.

'Would you rather have a glass of beer, or wine?'

He still resented these little traps of Maigret.

'No, thank you.'

'A sandwich?'

'Are you planning on keeping me here much longer?'

'I've no idea. It's possible. It depends on you.'

He went to the door and spoke to the inspectors.

'Could someone fetch me a road map of the Fontainebleau area?'

He took his time. This was nothing but words; he was just scratching the surface.

'When you go out for a bite, bring back some sandwiches and beers, Janvier.'

'OK, chief.'

Someone brought him the road map.

'Show me the spot where you stopped the car on Sunday.'

Serre looked at the map for a moment, picked up a pencil from the desk and marked a cross where the road crossed a country lane.

'If there is a farm with a red roof on the left, that's the right path.'

'How long were you walking for?'

'About a quarter of an hour.'

'Were you wearing the same shoes as today?'

He thought about this, looked at his shoes and nodded.

'Are you sure?'

'Positive.'

These shoes had rubber heels on which concentric circles had been imprinted around the name of the manufacturer.

'Don't you think, Monsieur Serre, that it would be a lot easier and less tiring for all concerned if you simply owned up? At what point did you kill your wife?'

'I didn't kill her.'

Maigret sighed and went to give more instructions next door. Too bad! This was going to take a few hours more. The dentist's complexion was looking a bit paler than in the morning, and he was starting to get rings under his eyes.

'Why did you marry her?'

'My mother advised me to.'

'For what reason?'

'She was afraid that I'd be left on my own one day. She thinks I am still a child and need someone to take care of me.'

'And to prevent you from drinking?'

Silence.

'So there was no love between you and Maria Van Aerts?'

'We were both of us touching fifty.'

'When did the arguments begin?'

'We never argued.'

'How did you spend your evenings, Monsieur Serre?'

'Me?'

'Yes, you.'

'Reading, mainly, in my study.'

'And your wife?'

'Writing, in her room. She went to bed early.'

'Did your father lose a lot of money?'

'I don't follow you.'

'Has anyone ever told you that your father used to lead a wild life?'

'He went out a lot.'

'Did he spend a lot?'

'I think so.'

'Did your mother make a scene about this?'

'We aren't the sort of people who make scenes.'

'How much did your first marriage net you?'

'I don't think we are speaking the same language.'

'Did you and your first wife marry under the laws of common property?'

'That is correct.'

'So she had a fortune. And you inherited it.'

'That's normal, isn't it?'

'As long as your second wife's body goes undiscovered, you won't be able to inherit from her.'

'Why wouldn't she be found alive?'

'Do you think she will, Serre?'

'I didn't kill her.'

'Why did you go out in your car on Tuesday evening?'

'I didn't.'

'The concierge of the building opposite saw you. It was around midnight.'

'You are forgetting that there are three garages, three former stables, whose doors adjoin each other. It was night time, as you yourself said. She could have been mistaken.'

'The shopkeeper at the hardware shop saw you in broad daylight, so could not have mistaken you for someone else, when you came to buy some putty and a second windowpane.'

'It's my word against his.'

'Provided that you didn't kill your wife. What did you do with the suitcases and the trunk?'

'It's the third time I've been asked this question. This time you forgot to mention the tools.'

'Where were you around midnight on Tuesday?'

'In my bed.'

'Are you a light sleeper, Monsieur Serre?'

'Me, no. My mother is.'

'Neither of you heard anything?'

'I believe I've already told you that.'

'And on Wednesday morning you found your house in order?'

'I suppose, since an official investigation is underway, that you have the right to question me. And you have decided to put me through a test of endurance, haven't you? Your colleague has already asked me these questions. Now you are starting all over again. I can see that this is likely to take all night. To save time, I will repeat once and for all that I did not kill my wife. I am also telling you that I will no longer give replies to questions I have already been asked. Is my mother here?'

'Do you have reason to think she is here?'

'Does that seem strange to you?'

'She is sitting in the waiting room.'

'Are you planning to keep her here all night?'

'I can't stop her. She is free to do as she wishes.'

This time, Guillaume Serre gave him a hate-filled look.

'I wouldn't like to do your job.'

'I wouldn't like to be in your shoes.'

They stared at each other in silence, neither wanting to break eye contact first.

'You killed your wife, Serre, just as, in all likelihood, you killed your first wife.'

Serre did not react.

'You will admit it in the end.'

The dentist's mouth curled into a contemptuous smile and he slumped back into his chair, crossing his legs.

Next door they could hear the sound of the waiter from the Brasserie Dauphine laying out plates and glasses on the desk.

'I will take up your offer of some food.'

'Do you wish to remove your jacket?'

'No.'

He started slowly eating a sandwich while Maigret went to the wash-basin in the closet to fill his glass.

It was eight o'clock in the evening.

The windows gradually got darker, and the view outside became reduced to pinpoints of light that seemed to be as distant as the stars.

Maigret had to send out for some more tobacco. At eleven o'clock, the dentist was smoking his last cigar, and the atmosphere was becoming more and more heavy. On two occasions Maigret went for a walk round the building and saw the two women in the waiting room. The second time, they had drawn their chairs closer together and were chatting away like two old friends.

'When did you last clean your car?'

'The last time it was cleaned was two weeks ago, in a garage in Neuilly, when I took it in for an oil change.'

'Has it been cleaned again since Sunday?'

'No.'

'You see, Monsieur Serre, we have just carried out a conclusive experiment. One of my inspectors, who, like you, was wearing rubber-heeled shoes, went to the crossing you pointed out on the Fontainebleau road. Just as you claimed to have done on Sunday with your mother, he got out of the car and walked down the country path. It was not paved. Then he got back into the car and returned here.

'Our experts in Criminal Records, who know their stuff, then examined the mat from the car.

'Here is the dust and gravel that they collected.'

He slid a paper bag across the desk.

Serre made no attempt to take the bag.

'We should have been able to collect the same amount of dust from the mat in your car.'

'And that proves that I killed my wife?'

'That proves that the car has been cleaned since Sunday.'

'Someone might have got into my garage.'

'That's unlikely.'

'Didn't your men get in?'

'What are you insinuating?'

'Nothing, inspector. I am not accusing anyone. I am only pointing out that your search took place without witnesses, hence with no legal safeguards.'

'Would you like to speak to your mother?'

'Would you like to know what I have to say to her? Nothing, Monsieur Maigret. I have nothing to say to her, and she has nothing to say to me.'

A thought suddenly crossed his mind.

'Has she had anything to eat?'

'I don't know. As I said, she is a free agent.'

'She won't leave as long as I am here.'

'Then she could be here a long time.'

Serre lowered his eyes and adopted a different tone. After a long pause, he murmured with what seemed like a touch of shame:

'I don't suppose I could ask you to take her a sandwich?'

'We did, quite some time ago.'

'Did she eat it?'

'Yes.'

'How is she?'

'She's busy talking.'

'To whom?'

'To another woman who is also sitting in the waiting room. A former lady of the night.'

Once again, the dentist's eyes flashed with hatred.

'You did it deliberately, didn't you?'

'Not at all.'

'My mother has nothing to say.'

'All the better for you.'

The following quarter of an hour passed in silence, then Maigret went wearily into the office next door, more irritable than ever, and waved to Janvier, who was snoozing in a corner.

'Same again, chief?'

'Whatever you like.'

The stenographer was exhausted. The translator was still at work in his cubby hole.

'Go and fetch Ernestine, the woman wearing the green hat, and bring her to me in Lucas' office.'

When La Grande Perche came in she didn't look too happy.

'You shouldn't have dragged me away. She will suspect something.'

Perhaps because the night was well advanced, Maigret was in no mood for niceties.

'What've you told her?'

'That I didn't know why I've been brought here, that my husband went away two days ago and I haven't had any news. That I hate the cops and all the stunts they try to pull.

'"They've kept me hanging around just to throw me off guard," I told her. "They think that they can get away with anything."'

'What did she say to that?'

'She asked me if I had been here before. I said yes, that I'd been interrogated for a whole night, about a year ago, because my husband had got into a fight in a café and someone had claimed he had drawn a knife. At first she looked at me like I was a piece of dirt. But little by little she started asking me questions.'

'About what?'

'Mainly about you. I painted as bad a picture as I could. I made sure to add that you always got people to talk, even if you had to use strong-arm tactics.'

'Huh?'

'I know what I'm doing. I mentioned that you'd once kept someone totally naked for twenty-four hours in your office in midwinter, with the window wide open.'

'That never happened.'

'No, but it made an impression on her. She's less sure of herself than when I first got here. She spends her whole time craning to hear.

'"Does he beat people up?" she asked me.

'"Sometimes."

'Do you want me to go back to her?'

'If you wish.'

'Only, it would be better if I was escorted back to the waiting room by an officer, and he handled me a bit roughly.'

'Still no news from Alfred?'

'No. You neither?'

Maigret had her led away as she had requested; the officer came back with a grin on his face.

'What happened?'

'Not a lot. When I walked past the old woman, she raised her arms as if she were expecting me to hit her. And no sooner was La Grande Perche out of your office than she burst into tears.'

Madame Maigret rang to see if her husband had eaten.

'Shall I wait up for you?'

'Definitely not.'

He had a headache. He was disgruntled with himself, with the others. Perhaps he was a little worried too. He wondered what would happen if they suddenly received a telephone call from Maria Van Aerts announcing that she had changed her plans and had installed herself in some town or other.

He drank a now lukewarm beer, ordered some more to be sent up before the brasserie closed and went back to his office, where Janvier had opened the window. The din of the city had subsided. Every now and again a taxi drove across Pont Saint-Michel.

He sat down, his shoulders slumped. Janvier went out. After a long silence, he said absently:

'Your mother thinks I am torturing you.'

He was surprised to see Serre jerk his head up, and for the first time he could see a worried look on his face.

'What have you been telling her?'

'I don't know. It's probably that woman she's talking to. People like her like to invent stories to make themselves appear interesting.'

'Can I see her?'

'Who?'

'My mother.'

Maigret pretended to hesitate, as if weighing up the pros and cons, then shook his head.

'No,' he decided. 'I think I'll interrogate her myself. And maybe I will fetch Eugénie in as well.'

'My mother knows nothing.'

'And you?'

'Neither do I.'

'Then there is no reason why I shouldn't interrogate her as I have interrogated you.'

'Have you no pity, inspector?'

'For whom?'

'For an old woman.'

'Maria would have liked to become an old woman too.'

He walked around the office with his hands behind his back, but what he was waiting for didn't happen.

'Over to you, Janvier! I'm off to have a go with the mother.'

In truth, he wasn't yet sure if he would or wouldn't. Later on, Janvier would recount that he had never seen the inspector as tired and surly as he was that night.

It was one o'clock in the morning. Everyone in the building had lost faith; behind Maigret's back, despairing looks were being exchanged.

8.

Maigret was leaving the inspectors' room to pay a visit to the translator when one of the men from the cleaning team, who had been at work for half an hour by now, came to tell him:

'There's a lady who wants to speak to you.'

'Where?'

'It's one of the two ladies who were in the waiting room. It seems she's not feeling very well. She came into the office I was sweeping, looking pale, like she was about to pass out, and asked me to come and tell you.'

'The old woman?' Maigret asked with a frown.

'No, the young one.'

Most of the doors along the corridor were open. In the second office along, Maigret saw Ernestine with her hand on her chest. He walked quickly towards her, with a serious expression and a question forming on his lips.

'Close the door,' she whispered when he got closer.

And once he had done that:

'Phew! I had to get out, but not because I'm sick. I just put it on to have an excuse to escape for a few minutes.

Not that I feel that great, by the way. Do you have a proper drink anywhere?'

He had to return to his office to fetch a bottle of cognac he always kept in his cupboard. Not having proper glasses, he poured some out into a tumbler, and she knocked it back in one go and gagged slightly.

'I don't know how you're getting on with the son, but I've had it up to here with the mother. My head was spinning by the end.'

'Did she talk?'

'She's cleverer than me. That's what I wanted to tell you. At the start, I was convinced that she'd swallowed all the fibs I came out with.

'Then, I can't remember how it started, she began asking me these little, innocent-sounding questions. I've had the third degree before, so I thought I was well up to defending myself.

'But she played me for a fool.'

'Did you tell her who you were?'

'Not exactly. That woman is frighteningly intelligent, Monsieur Maigret. How did she guess that I've worked the streets? Tell me that. Is it really still that obvious? Because she said to me:

'"You've had experience of these people, haven't you?"

'By "these people" she meant you lot.

'Eventually she asked me about life in prison, and I answered her.

'If you'd told me when I first sat down opposite her that I'd be the one spilling the beans, I wouldn't have believed you.'

'Did you talk to her about Alfred?'

'Sort of. Without mentioning what he does. She thinks he's a money-launderer. That's not really what interests her. She's been asking about life in prison for at least three-quarters of an hour: what time do you get up? How do the warders treat you? . . . I thought you'd be interested to know about that, so I made out I was feeling sick. I got up and told her I was going to get something to drink and complained that it was inhuman to keep women hanging around all night . . .'

'Could I have another slug?'

She was really tired. The drink brought some colour back into her cheeks.

'Is the son talking?'

'Not yet. Has she mentioned him at all?'

'She's listening out to every sound. She gives a start every time a door opens. She asked me another question. She wanted to know if I have ever known anyone who was sent to the guillotine. Right, now I'm feeling a bit better, I'll go back to her. I'll be on my guard this time, don't worry.'

She took the opportunity to apply some face powder. She looked at the bottle but didn't dare ask for a third drink.

'What time is it?'

'Three o'clock.'

'I don't know how she does it. She doesn't look the slightest bit tired, and she's sitting as bolt upright as at the start of the evening.'

Maigret allowed her to pass, took a breath of air at a window opening on to the courtyard well and drank a mouthful of cognac from the bottle. When he passed by the office where the translator was working, the latter showed him a passage in a letter that he had underlined.

'This is from a year and a half ago,' he said.

Maria wrote to her friend:

I had a good laugh yesterday. G was in my room – not for the reason you think, but to talk to me about a plan I had made the previous evening to go to Nice for a couple of days.

Those two hate travelling. Apart from one single occasion they have never left France. The only time they ever travelled abroad was when the father was still alive and they all went to London together. It seems they were all seasick, and the ship's doctor had to attend to them.

But that's not what this is about. Whenever I say anything that displeases them they don't respond straight away. They stay silent and, as the saying goes, you can hear a pin drop.

So, later or the next day, G comes to see me in my room, looking a bit put out, beats about the bush a bit and finally spits out what is bothering him. In short, it seems my idea of going to Nice for the Carnival is absurd, almost indecent. He made no bones about the fact that his mother was shocked and was begging me to change my mind.

Now it just so happens that the drawer of my bedside table was slightly open. He gave it a cursory glance, and then I saw him turn quite pale.

'What's that?' he stammered, pointing to the small pistol with the mother-of-pearl handle that I had bought on my trip to Egypt.

Do you remember? I told you about it at the time. I had been warned that a woman on her own is not safe in those countries.

I don't know why I had put it in the drawer. I said quite calmly:

'It's a revolver.'

'Is it loaded?'

'I can't remember.'

I picked it up and checked if it was loaded. There were no bullets in it.

'Do you have any ammunition?'

'I must do somewhere.'

Half an hour later my mother-in-law showed up on some pretext or other. She too beat around the bush before she came out and told me that it was not the done thing for a woman to possess a firearm.

'But it's little more than a toy,' I replied. 'I've kept it as a souvenir, because it has a pretty handle and has my initials engraved on it. I don't think it would do anyone any great harm.'

In the end she gave way. But not before I had handed over the box of ammunition that I had at the back of the drawer.

The funny thing was, no sooner had she left the room than I found another packet of bullets, which I had forgotten about, in one of my handbags. I didn't tell her about that . . .

Maigret still had the bottle of cognac in his hand and he poured out a drink for the translator, then went and gave some to the stenographer and to another inspector, who was trying to stay awake by doodling stick men on his blotter.

He returned to his office, which Janvier vacated on cue. And so began the next round.

'I've been having a think, Serre. I'm beginning to conclude that you haven't been lying as much as I thought you were.'

He had dropped the 'Monsieur', as if, after hours of face-to-face talking, they had developed a certain familiarity. The dentist continued to eye him distrustfully.

'You didn't intend Maria to disappear any more than your first wife. You have no interest in her disappearing. She had packed her bags and had announced that she was heading back to Holland. She had every intention of taking the night train.

'I don't know if she was meant to die in the house or once she was outside. What are your thoughts about that?'

Guillaume Serre didn't reply, but his face was showing distinct signs of interest.

'If you prefer, she was meant to die a natural death, by which I mean a death that *could be passed off* as natural.

'But that's not what happened, otherwise you would have had no reason to dispose of her body and her luggage.

'There is another detail that doesn't quite fit. You had said your goodbyes. So she had no reason to go back into your study. Yet her body was seen in there later that night.

'I'm not asking you to reply, just to follow my reasoning. I have just learned that your wife possessed a pistol.

'I'd be prepared to believe that you used it to defend yourself. Then, seized by panic, you left the body where it lay while you went to the garage to fetch your car. It was at that moment, around midnight, that the concierge spotted you.

'What I am trying to understand is: what happened to change your plans and hers? You were in your study, is that correct?'

'I don't recall.'

'You told me that you were.'

'Maybe I did.'

'I am convinced that your mother was not in her room but was with you.'

'She was in her room.'

'You remember that?'

'Yes.'

'So you also remember that you were in your study? Your wife hadn't yet gone out to find a taxi. If she had hailed a taxi that night, we would have tracked down the driver. In other words, before leaving the house, she changed her plan and came to your study. Why?'

'I don't know.'

'Do you acknowledge that she came to see you?'

'No.'

'You're making a mistake, Serre. There are very few cases in the criminal records where a body was not found sooner or later. We will find hers. I am now convinced that the post-mortem will show that she was killed by one or two bullets. What I am asking myself is whether the bullet came from your gun or hers.

'The answer to that will determine the seriousness of this case. If the bullet was from her gun, it would imply that, for one reason or another, she decided to go and settle accounts with you and threatened you.

'Was it about money, Serre?'

He shrugged his shoulders.

'You rush at her, disarm her but press the trigger without meaning to. Another hypothesis is that she threatened your mother, not you. A woman can more easily hate another woman than a man.

'A final hypothesis is that your own revolver was not in your room, where you placed it a short time afterwards, but in a drawer of your desk.

'Maria comes in. She is armed. She threatens you. You open the drawer and shoot first.

'In all these cases, no death penalty would apply. There is no question of premeditation, as it is quite normal to keep a revolver in a desk drawer.

'You could even plead self-defence.

'What remains to be explained is why your wife, as she was about to leave, should come at you with a gun in her hand.'

He leaned back and slowly filled his pipe without taking his eyes off Serre.

'What do you think about that?'

'This is likely to take a while,' said Serre with a sort of disgust.

'Are you still insisting on saying nothing?'

'I am obediently answering your questions.'

'You haven't told me why you pulled the trigger.'

'I didn't do that.'

'So it was your mother?'

'Not my mother either. She was in her room.'

'While you were having a discussion with your wife?'

'There was no discussion.'

'That's a shame.'

'I'm sorry.'

'You see, Serre, I have searched hard for a reason why Maria might have wanted to settle accounts with you and threaten you.'

'She didn't threaten me.'

'I wouldn't state that too categorically, as you might regret it later on. You will be trying to convince me or the jurors that your life or your mother's life was at stake.'

Serre gave an ironic smile. He was tired, his posture was slumped, his shoulders were hunched around his neck, but he had lost nothing of his self-possession. His cheeks were blue with stubble. The sky outside the window was less dark now, and the air in the room had grown cooler.

Maigret felt the cold first and went to close the window.

'It wasn't in your interest to have a corpse on your hands. *I mean a corpse that no one could be allowed to see.* Do you follow me?'

'No.'

'When your first wife died, the circumstances were such that you could call Doctor Dutilleux to write the death certificate.

'That's how Maria was meant to die, apparently from natural causes. She too had a heart condition. What worked for one should have worked for the other.

'But there was a snag.

'Do you see now what I am getting at?'

'I didn't kill her.'

'And you didn't dispose of her body along with her luggage and the burglar's tools?'

'There was no burglar.'

'I will probably be introducing him to you in a few hours.'

'You've found him?'

There was a hint of worry in his voice.

'We found his fingerprints in your study. You took great care to wipe all the surfaces, but there is always somewhere that you miss. He is a repeat offender, a safe specialist well known to the police: Alfred Jussiaume, known as Sad Freddie. He told his wife what he had seen. She is currently sitting in the waiting room outside with your mother. As for Jussiaume, he is in Rouen and has no further need to hide.

'We already have the concierge, who saw you take your car out of the garage. We also have the man from the hardware shop who sold you a second windowpane at eight o'clock on Wednesday morning.

'Criminal Records will verify that your car has been cleaned since then.

'That is a lot of circumstantial evidence, no?

'Once we find the body and the luggage, my work will be complete.

'So perhaps you might consider explaining why, instead of what we might call a legitimate corpse, you were lumbered with a body that you had to get rid of as a matter of urgency.

'There was some hitch.

'What was it, Serre?'

The man took a handkerchief from his pocket, wiped his lips and brow but didn't open his mouth to speak.

'It is half past three. I'm beginning to get fed up. Are you still refusing to speak?'

'I have nothing to say.'

'Very well,' said Maigret as he got up. 'It pains me to torment an old woman, but I have no choice but to question your mother.'

He was expecting a protest, or some sort of reaction at least. The dentist didn't turn a hair. Maigret even thought that he looked relieved, that his nerves relaxed.

'Over to you, Janvier. I am going to try the mother.'

And he intended to! But he couldn't do this straight away, because Vacher had just arrived in a state of excitement, with a package in his hand.

'I found it, chief! It took a while, but I think I've got it.'

He undid the bundle of newspaper to reveal some bits of brick and some reddish dust.

'Where?'

'Quai de Billancourt, opposite Ile Seguin. If I'd started downstream rather than upstream, I'd have been back hours ago. I covered all the unloading docks. Only Billancourt had a barge deliver a cargo of bricks recently.'

'When?'

'Last Monday. The boat left on Tuesday around midday. The bricks are still stacked there, and some kids must have been playing on them and broken a few. There is red dust scattered over a large part of the dock. Shall I take it up to Moers?'

'I'll take it myself.'

As he passed the waiting room, he looked at the two women, who weren't talking. From their attitudes it seemed as if things had turned a little frosty between them.

Maigret went into the laboratory, where Moers had just brewed some coffee, a cup of which came his way.

'Do you have the brick sample? Can you make a comparison?'

The colour was the same, the grain almost identical. Moers used a microscope and a projector.

'Is it a match?'

'Very likely. In any case, it comes from the same region. I'll need about half an hour to an hour to do the analysis.'

It was too late to search the Seine. It would be sunrise before the river police would be able to send a diver down. Then, if they found Maria's body, or just the suitcases and the toolbox, the circle would be closed.

'Hello! River police? Maigret here.'

He still seemed to be in a bad mood.

'I'd like you to search the Seine as soon as possible, Quai de Billancourt, at the spot where some bricks have been unloaded recently.'

'An hour from now it will be daylight.'

What was stopping him from waiting? A jury wouldn't need any more evidence to convict Guillaume Serre, who would continue to deny everything.

Ignoring the stenographer, who was looking at him, Maigret drank a whole measure straight from the bottle, wiped his mouth, went out into the corridor and threw open the door to the waiting room.

Ernestine thought it was her he had come for and sat up. Madame Serre didn't move.

It was the latter whom he addressed:

'Would you come with me for a moment?'

He had a corridor of empty offices to choose from. He opened a door at random, closed the window.

'Please, sit down.'

He started circling the room, casting a surly look at the old woman.

'I don't like giving bad news,' he eventually growled. 'Especially not to someone of your age. Have you ever been ill, Madame Serre?'

'Apart from a bout of seasickness when we crossed the Channel, I have never had need of a doctor.'

'And of course you don't have a heart condition?'

'No.'

'Your son does, though, doesn't he?'

'He has always had a slightly enlarged heart.'

'He killed his wife!' he said, lifting his head and staring her straight in the face.

'Did he tell you that?'

He hated having recourse to the old trick of the false confession.

'He continues to deny it, but it won't do him any good. We have proof.'

'That he killed her?'

'That he shot Maria in his study.'

She hadn't moved. Her expression had somewhat frozen, she seemed to be holding her breath, but she was showing no other signs of emotion.

'What proof do you have?'

'We have found the spot where his wife's body was thrown into the Seine, along with her luggage and the burglar's tools.'

'Ah!'

She didn't add anything. She just waited, hands clasped on her dark dress.

'Your son refuses to claim he was acting in self-defence. He's making a mistake, because I am convinced that, when his wife came into his study, she did so with malicious intent.'

'Why?'

'That's what I'm asking you.'

'I know nothing.'

'Where were you?'

'I've told you: in my room.'

'And you didn't hear anything?'

'Not a thing. Just the door closing. Then the sound of the car engine out in the street.'

'The taxi?'

'I presume it was a taxi, since my daughter-in-law had talked of going to find one.'

'So you're not sure? It could have been a private car?'

'I didn't see it.'

'Could it have been your son's car?'

'He told me that he hadn't taken it out.'

'Are you aware that there are discrepancies between the answers you are giving now and the statement you made when you came to see me out of the blue?'

'No.'

'You were sure that your daughter-in-law had left in a taxi.'

'I still think she did.'

'But you aren't certain. Nor are you certain that there was no attempted break-in.'

'I saw no trace of it.'

'What time did you get up on Wednesday morning?'

'Around six thirty.'

'Did you go into the study?'

'Not straight away. I made some coffee.'

'You didn't go in to open the windows?'

'Yes, I think I did.'

'Before your son came down?'

'Possibly.'

'You won't confirm that?'

'Put yourself in my place, Monsieur Maigret. For the last two days I haven't known whether I'm coming or going. I've been asked all sorts of questions. I've been sitting out in that waiting room for God knows how long. I'm tired. I'm doing all I can just to keep going.'

'Why did you come here tonight?'

'Any mother would follow her son under these circumstances, wouldn't she? I've always been by his side. He might need me.'

'Would you follow him all the way to prison?'

'I don't understand. I don't think that—'

'Let me put it another way: if I charged your son, would you take some of the responsibility for his actions?'

'But he hasn't done anything!'

'Are you sure of that?'

'Why would he have killed his wife?'

'You're avoiding the question. Are you absolutely certain that he didn't kill her?'

'As far as I know.'

'Is it possible that he could have done?'

'He had no reason to.'

'He did it,' he said harshly, staring her in the face.

It was as if she were in suspended animation. Then she said:

'Ah!'

She opened her bag and took out her handkerchief. Her eyes were dry. She wasn't crying. She settled for wiping her mouth with it.

'Could I have a glass of water?'

He had to look round for a moment, as the office wasn't as familiar to him as his own.

'As soon as the public prosecutor arrives for work at the Palais de Justice your son will be charged. I can tell you now that he hasn't the slightest chance of getting off.'

'You mean he—'

'He will pay with his head.'

She didn't faint, but sat rigidly in her chair, her eyes fixed ahead of her.

'His first wife's body will be exhumed. You are no doubt aware that traces of certain poisons can be lifted even from a skeleton.'

'Why would he have killed both of them? It defies belief. It's simply not true, inspector. I don't know why you are saying these things to me but I refuse to believe you. Let me speak to him face to face and I will get to the bottom of it.'

'Did you spend the whole of Tuesday in your room?'

'Yes.'

'Did you come downstairs at any point?'

'No. Why would I have come downstairs, since that woman was leaving us at last?'

Maigret pressed his head against the window for a while, then went into the office next door, grabbed the bottle and drank the equivalent of three or four small glasses.

When he came back he had the heavy tread and stubborn look of Guillaume Serre himself.

9.

In which Maigret is not proud of his work but nevertheless derives satisfaction from saving someone's life

He was sitting in someone else's chair, both elbows on the table, his chunkiest pipe in his mouth, staring at this woman he had once compared to a mother superior.

'Your son, Madame Serre, killed neither his first wife nor his second wife,' he said, enunciating each syllable clearly.

She frowned, surprised, but there was no joy in her look.

'Nor did he kill his father,' he added.

'What . . . ?'

'Shush! . . . If I may, we can tidy this matter up once and for all. We won't worry about proof for now – that will come in due course.

'We won't get too hung up on the case of your husband either. I am almost certain your first daughter-in-law was poisoned. I'll go further. I am convinced that it wasn't arsenic or any of the other toxic poisons traditionally used in these cases.

'I should mention in passing, Madame Serre, that poisonings are, nine times out of ten, the work of women.

'Your first daughter-in-law, like your second, suffered from a heart condition. As did your husband.

'Certain drugs that are harmless to a person in good health can be life-threatening to a person with heart problems. I am wondering if the key to the puzzle is in one of the letters that Maria wrote to her friend. She spoke of a journey you made with your husband to England and emphasized that you were all so seasick that the ship's doctor had to be called.

'What is prescribed in cases like this?'

'I don't know.'

'I find that hard to believe. Usually they give atropine in one form or another. Too large a dose of atropine can be fatal to a person with a bad heart.'

'You mean that my husband—'

'We'll come back to that, even if it turns out to be impossible to prove. In his later years your husband led a dissolute life and spent a great deal of his fortune. You have always lived in fear of penury, Madame Serre.'

'Not on my own behalf, but my son's. That doesn't mean that I would have—'

'Later, your son got married. There was another woman living in your house, a woman who, at a stroke, bore the same name and had the same rights as you.'

She pursed her lips.

'This woman, who also had a weak heart, was rich, richer than your son, richer than all the Serres put together.'

'Are you saying that I poisoned her, having poisoned my own husband?'

'Yes.'

She gave a little forced laugh.

'And no doubt I poisoned my second daughter-in-law too?'

'She left, demoralized, having tried in vain to live in a household in which she was perpetually an outsider. She probably took her money with her. By chance, she also had a weak heart.

'You see, from the start I have been wondering why her body disappeared. If she had simply been poisoned, all you needed to do was to call a doctor, who, given Maria's medical history, would have diagnosed a heart attack. Perhaps this attack was meant to occur later, in the taxi, at the station or on the train.'

'You seem very sure of yourself, Monsieur Maigret.'

'I know that some event took place that forced your son to shoot his wife. Perhaps Maria, as she was about to go to find a taxi or, as is more likely, to telephone to order one, started to experience certain symptoms.

'She knew both of you well, having lived with you for two and a half years. She had read a lot on a wide range of subjects, and I wouldn't be surprised if she had picked up some medical knowledge.

'Realizing that she had been poisoned, she went into your son's study, and you were there.'

'How can you be so sure that I was there?'

'Because it was you that she blamed – fatally for her, as it turned out. If you had been in your room, she would have come upstairs.

'I don't know whether she threatened you with her revolver or whether she simply reached out for the telephone in order to inform the police . . .

'You had no other option than to shoot her.'

'And, according to you, it was I who—'

'No. I've already said that it was probably your son who fired; if you like, he did your dirty work for you.'

A smudge of dawn was mingling with the light of the lamps, and in it their features seemed more deeply etched. The telephone rang loudly.

'Is that you, chief? I've completed the analysis. It's almost certain that the brick dust taken from the car comes from Billancourt.'

'You can go to bed now, my friend. Your work is done.'

He got up again and began circling the room.

'Your son, Madame Serre, has taken all the blame on himself. I see no way to dissuade him. If he has managed to hold his tongue all through this night, he will be able to do so right to the end. Unless . . .'

'Unless . . . ?'

'I don't know. I was thinking out loud. Two years ago I had a man as tough as him in my office. For fifteen hours we didn't get a word out of him.'

He gave the window a violent tug, as if he was in a rage.

'It took us twenty-seven and a half hours to break him down.'

'Did he talk?'

'He told us everything, without pausing for breath, spilled his guts.'

'I didn't poison anyone.'

'It's not you I need the answer from.'

'My son?'

'Yes. He is convinced that you did what you did only for his sake, half out of a fear of seeing him left without resources, half out of jealousy.'

He had to restrain himself from giving her a slap, despite her age, because an involuntary smile had crept across the old woman's mouth.

'But that's not true!' he asserted.

He came up close to her, stared into her eyes, his breath on her face, and barked:

'It's not for his sake that you are afraid of poverty, but yours! It's not for his sake that you killed. The real reason you are here tonight is that you were scared that he would tell all.'

She tried to recoil, to sit back in her chair, because Maigret's face was right in hers, hard and menacing.

'It doesn't matter if he goes to prison, or even if he is executed, as long as you escape scot free. You are sure that you have many more years to live, sitting in your house, counting your money . . .'

She was afraid. Her mouth opened as if to call for help. Suddenly Maigret did something unexpected; he forcefully wrenched her hands away from the bag that she had been clinging on to.

She cried out, jumped up to retrieve it.

'Sit down!'

He undid the silver clasp. At the bottom, under the gloves, under the purse, under the handkerchief and compact, he found a folded piece of paper containing two white pills.

A hush descended, as in a church or a cave. Maigret let his body unwind, sat down and pressed an electric buzzer.

When the door opened, without glancing at the officer, he said:

'Tell Janvier to let him go.'

And then, as the officer stood there, dumbfounded:

'It's over. She has confessed.'

'I haven't confessed to anything.'

He waited until the door closed again.

'It's the same thing in the end. I could have seen the experiment through to the end, given you the one-to-one meeting with your son that you asked for. Don't you think there have been enough corpses already, for one old lady?'

'Are you suggesting that I would have . . . ?'

He toyed with the pills.

'You would have given him his medicine, or more precisely what he would have assumed was his medicine, and there would be no more risk of him talking.'

The rooftops were beginning to be crested by daylight. The telephone rang again.

'Detective Chief Inspector Maigret? River police here. We are at Billancourt. The diver has been down and has discovered a heavy trunk.'

'The rest will be there too,' he said without curiosity.

Janvier appeared in the doorway, looking exhausted and surprised.

'I was told—'

'Take her to the cells. The man too, for being an accessory. I'll see the public prosecutor as soon as he gets in.'

He had nothing more to do with either the mother or the son.

'You can go to bed now,' he told the translator.

'Is it over?'

'For today.'

The dentist wasn't there by the time he got back to his office, but there were some very dark cigar butts in his ashtray. He sat down in his chair and was about to nod off when he remembered La Grande Perche.

He found her in the waiting room, asleep. He shook her shoulder and, instinctively, straightened her green hat.

'It's over. You can go home now.'

'Did he confess?'

'It was her.'

'What? You mean the old woman—'

'Later,' he murmured.

Then, with a pang of conscience, he turned round and said:

'And thank you! When Alfred comes home, advise him to . . .'

What was the use? Nothing was going to deflect Sad Freddie from his obsession with burgling the safes he himself had installed, or his conviction that the next one was going to be the last, and this time he would really end up living in the country.

Because of her age, old Madame Serre was not sentenced to death and left court with the satisfied look of someone who was going to bring some long-overdue order to the women's prison.

When her son got out of Fresnes, after two years, he went straight back to the house in Rue de la Ferme and, that very evening, went on that same walk he used to go on when he had a dog to exercise.

He continued to drink red wine in the little bar and every time, before he went in, he would glance anxiously up and down the street.